"A funny, scrambling caper about a widow whose only regret is that her husband didn't leave her sooner—or leave her more."

Chicago Sun-Times

"Reading *The Pew Group* is the most fun I've had since my first Agatha Christie or E.F. Benson. . . . pure delight for fans of English mysteries."

Memphis Commercial Appeal

"For sheer, glorious fun and surprises, Welsh author Oliver's first novel is hard to beat from the moment it takes off."

Publishers Weekly

"Naughty, comical, slightly arch doings in an English village . . . considerable stylish fun—with more than a few moments of truly inspired, deadpan hilarity."

The Kirkus Reviews

"A civilized, even absorbing piece of work . . . a skillful and sensitive writer."

Newgate Callendar
The New York Times Book
Review

THE PEW GROUP

ANTHONY OLIVER

FAWCETT CREST • NEW YORK

A Fawcett Crest Book
Published by Ballantine Books
Copyright © 1980 by Anthony Oliver

Library of Congress Catalog Card Number: 80-2079
ISBN 0-449-20594-0
This edition published by arrangement with Doubleday and Company, Inc.

Manufactured in the United States of America

First Ballantine Books Edition: May 1985

CHAPTER 1

YOU COULDN'T CALL it murder and she had no intention of doing so. But the fact remained that at 9:51 P.M. her husband was alive and reasonably well at the top of the stairs, and that seven seconds later he was lying rather awkwardly a few feet beyond the bottom step and beyond all spiritual or medical aid. From the bedroom came a great cheering roar of applause as the television commentator confirmed a clear round for Harvey Smith. By the time the doctor arrived, which was not until after the show jumping had finished at 10:50, she had dressed in a light-weight blue linen trouser suit that she had chosen as suitable both for Spain and for Saturday morning shopping in Flaxfield. She had also covered Rupert's body with a blanket from the spare bedroom because in the summer they neither of them wore anything in bed, and somehow she felt that the doctor might expect a man of his age to wear pyjamas or at least underpants.

That he was dead she could have no doubt. She hadn't been able to bring herself to touch him to feel for the pulse, but the little mirror she had used to adjust her unsuitable make-up remained clear and unclouded. What made it quite certain in her mind was the angle of the head on his shoulders. Sometimes when people had brought some interesting old piece into the shop to sell, she had seen his head bend appreciatively to the left as he assessed it for beauty and profit, but never as far as this, and in any case it was now bending sharply to the right, a direction she had never seen it take in life whatever treasure had appeared before him.

She drew the blanket over the nearly bald head, covering the open brown eyes gazing upwards with surprise at an old damp patch in the corner of the ceiling. Apart from his neck the only thing which suffered any damage was a small Staffordshire pottery figure of Queen Victoria which had shared the same fate but could be restored. She replaced the two pieces on the telephone table at the foot of the stairs half expecting her mother to ring. There was no reason why she should except that her mother always chose the most inconvenient moments to talk about her legs. Another burst of cheering from the television set in the bedroom reminded her that as long as the show jumping lasted her mother wouldn't phone.

Doreen sat at the foot of the bed seeing the reflection of her naked body in the television set cover almost the whole of the show jumping course. It wasn't that she was gross or fat, at thirty-five she still had a reasonable figure, but although it was a colour set the screen was small, not like the huge one in their sitting room downstairs behind the shop in which she would have appeared quite petite. She wanted to climb into bed and cover herself for comfort but it was still warm and she chose to shiver with shock and excitement until she dressed before telephoning for Doctor Maguire. Rupert quite liked Doctor Maguire, they were much the same age and friendly, but it didn't matter anymore what Rupert thought. Round after round of riders plunged and shied around the stadium, disappearing through her left breast and emerging triumphantly through her stomach or between her legs, sometimes scattering poles or bricks over her thighs. It seemed odd that it should all go on as if nothing had happened.

Poor Rupert, and she had tried to warn him. She felt it had been meant as a sort of warning, although of course she had had no idea of what was going to happen. How could she? It certainly hadn't been planned and she certainly had tried to stop him. Almost from the day she allowed her mother to persuade her to accept Rupert's proposal of marriage she had regretted it and dreamed of freedom, but dreaming wasn't planning. She hadn't even hated him strongly, she had just wished very much that he wasn't there. Not in their bed, which she had never ceased to occupy in duty and boredom, not watching television and drinking too much whisky, even though she had never seen him really drunk, and not in the shop, where he sold some of the most beautiful antiques in Suffolk, many of them quite genuine.

A girl with a bottom broadened and battered into insensibility by a thousand saddles since the age of 6 sailed effortlessly over the first and easiest fence but without her horse who had decided at the last second to make his protest early on. You could see he hadn't planned it either; that was simply the way it had happened.

"Surely you've had enough whisky to make you sleep well already?"

"There wasn't all that much left. I'll just pop down and get another bottle; besides there's nearly another hour of this yet."

Another hour, another week, and then stretching on before her for as long as she could think of. Because he liked to watch television in bed and drink. In her mind the bottle had danger marks on it. Two to three inches was safe and cheerful and a useful time to extract promises and favours, between three and six inches was a danger time for sex, over six saved her from that but usually meant a restless night for her, listening to him snoring. Tonight, so far, he had drunk about four inches and another hour of television lay ahead which certainly wouldn't stop him—indeed, in some curious way the bright chattering screen seemed to stimulate him almost as much as the whisky. Through the years she had assumed some very odd positions in front of most of the news readers, party political broadcasts, and the Archbishop of Canterbury. Doreen read the look on her husband's face with accuracy and resignation. Only whisky and sex, Rupert decided, could compensate him for his bitter disappointment.

That afternoon in a private house he had seen something of such stupendous rarity that he couldn't believe his eyes, and he had failed to buy it. It was an old problem: the woman had no idea what she owned. Should he offer her a high price to tempt her? Or a low price to disguise its value? If he'd gone high the woman may well have panicked and had it valued. So he'd gone low and the stupid bitch had turned him down.

"We could do with more water too."

As she came back from the bathroom with the Irish crystal jug of water she found herself exactly one pace behind him as he reached the top of the stairs, as his right foot swung forward, confidently expecting to pass his left, she deftly diverted it with her toe on to his left ankle. He disappeared without a sound until he landed near the telephone table, and she hadn't spilled a single drop of water.

* * *

Doctor Maguire was very kind, and the men who came to take Rupert away in the ambulance. All the neighbours were shocked and kind, and all their friends and customers who had known them as a happy and devoted couple.

The coroner, Doctor Maguire, who was also a customer, was tactful, eliciting gently from Doreen, Rupert's drinking habits to underline the evidence of the post mortem.

"Of course that was only at home, never if he was driving."

"Quite so, quite so. I myself can vouch for what you say Mrs. Corder."

He wondered if Rupert kept accurate notes of his transactions. He suspected that he did. Although the shop was fairly successful, Maguire knew from his chats with Corder through the years that times were often quite hard in the antique trade and the Corders lived very modestly. Almost certainly, then, there would be a note that he still owed Corder some three hundred pounds on that very handsome Regency sofa table. He decided to say nothing until Corder's business affairs had been sorted out and recommended the jury to return a verdict of accidental death, adding that he was sure she had the sympathy of everyone in the court.

"Is that Flaxfield seven two zero?"

Doreen eased off her left shoe with her right letting the blood flow into the pinched veins so that the throbbing became almost a pleasure. They were the only pair of black shoes that she had and her left foot had always been a problem.

"Yes it is."

"A Mrs. Thomas is calling from Cardiff and wishes you to pay for the call. Will you accept the charge?"

No better way could describe a telephone call from her mother, she was as formidable as the Light Brigade at Balaclava. From Glamorgan, across the valleys of Gwent and the amazed fields of England, Mrs. Thomas volleyed and thundered into her daughter's ear.

". . . that was on the Thursday and then I had to tell her twice before she could take it in, you know how slow she can be. Edith, I said, it's not the same, that was in the war and you never saw it happen. Think of it! I said, a girl of thirty-two, stark naked with a jug full of water and her husband dead at her feet."

"Thirty-five."

"What?"

"I'm thirty-five Mam, and I was dressed when the doctor came, it all came out at the inquest, so when you come up next time don't go saying . . ."

"No, no of course love, quite right, now listen . . ."

Mrs. Thomas rallied her forces. Doreen kicked off her other shoe and listened wondering, as she had so often before, how she could stem the flow. No, she really had no idea how the business stood financially or even how much there was in the bank. It would all have to be sorted out.

"Mam, I don't think this is the cheap rate, so we mustn't be too long. So now, don't worry about the funeral—everyone's ever so kind. I'll be all right, honest I will. Yes of course I can manage, I had to when he was off buying didn't I? and all the prices are marked and everything."

"What are you going to wear?"

"Same as I wore for Dada. I wore it this morning for the inquest, no sense in buying new, I might have to be careful."

"Shall I send you the black straw I had dyed for Auntie Gwen? No one's seen it up there."

Doreen shuddered; nor would they if she could help it.

"No thanks Mam. Look, I must go, there's so much to do."

"All right my lovely, try not to cry too much, remember your mam loves you."

Now Doreen did cry, quite suddenly without expecting to.

"I'll be all right, 'bye."

"Doreen!" The wires flinched and tightened across the country.

"What?"

"Remember you're thirty-two in Cardiff."

On the day of the inquest the curate of St. Peter's in Flaxfield, the Reverend Michael Sabini, cycled through the lanes on the east of the town on his way to help with the village fête in the neighbouring parish of Lower Henworth. The fête, in aid of St. Paul's Church Organ Fund, had been opened that morning by Lady Ormundham with the support of two sticks and the vicar, the television personality having been, at the last moment, regrettably unable to keep his promise, a broken pledge he would later regret a great deal more. There are many churches in Suffolk and not enough clergy to go round, so the vicar was now back in Flaxfield listening with increasing gloom to the architect's report on the roof of St. Peter's, and Michael Sabini, his distant Italian ancestry promoting a pleasant tan on his handsome face, cycled through the June sunshine to do battle with the ladies of Lower Henworth.

On a slight rise to the north of the field in which the fête was being held, Joseph O'Shea guided his horse and cart into the shade of an over-hanging willow tree. Gently relieving himself of the beer he had drunk with his cheese and pickle sandwiches in the Henworth Arms at lunch time, he washed quite a lot of the white road dust from the cow parsley and buttercups in the hedgerow as the recorded music of Scott Joplin's *Rag Time Dance* floated invitingly up to him from the field below. He might strike it lucky here. You could spend a whole day knocking on cottage doors for miles around and not do so well as the junk stalls at a village fête, wasn't that the truth? Chamber pots with frogs inside and printed with rude verses, sets of old cigarette cards and once, only a few weeks ago, a broken old barometer that an antique dealer had given him ten pounds for only hours later.

Miss Hislop surveyed her stall gloomily. Really it was too bad, this was the second year she had been landed with the Bring and Buy and whatever Mrs. Willow said at the committee meeting ("Such charming old things, and you have such a gift for selling Mary, I know you'll do well"), it was junk, just dirty old junk. An excuse for everyone to dump their old rubbish on her. Mary Hislop would have much preferred to sell nice clean jars of home-made jam and real lemon curd, but she had been over-ruled. Nevertheless, with innocence and love in her heart for St. Paul's Church Lower Henworth and the Reverend Michael Sabini, she had done her best. Her stall was bright with roses from her garden, and as much of her stock as could be washed she had done herself in the kitchen sink, before labelling and pricing each piece as accurately and optimistically as she dared with fingers which had felt the first premature twinges of rheumatism last winter. Her finest effort, of which she was most proud, was a notice propped up against a teapot with a chipped lid. It was executed with felt markers in green and purple. "Bring and Buy!" it exhorted. "St. Paul's Organ is Worn Out. Please help the Vicar."

Chapter 2

Doreen sat at Rupert's desk in the alcove at the back of the shop which had served him as an office. An untidy pile of letters lay on the desk; some of them had been opened by Rupert before the accident, some she had opened herself. All of them would have to be answered, and very few of them made much sense to her. She was perfectly capable of running the shop and had often done so when he was away, sometimes for quite long periods. Through the years she had picked up a useful smattering of knowledge simply by listening to him talking to customers and, when her own interest in something had been aroused, by asking him questions which he had always answered carefully if somewhat briefly. Answers as neat and condensed as the descriptions he had written on the little tie-on tickets attached to everything in the shop, each one of which bore the printed name "Rupert Corder Fine Antiques" at the top, and the assurance "Guaranteed Genuine" at the bottom.

On some of the letters Rupert had opened he had written

a few words indicating his reply. *Answered June 2nd £300–£400 depending upon date and condition. Answered June 4th Thank you don't want it.* All these she had placed in a separate pile and stared bereft at the others, the full implications of her new found widowhood, combining with the hot June sunshine slanting across the shop, gave her a sweaty sense of unease she had not felt since she had been caught cheating at O levels. But Doreen was not her mother's daughter for nothing. Bugger them, she thought, reaching for Rupert's pen. I'll learn.

With lesser problems to worry about, although they did not seem so to her, Miss Hislop at the Bring and Buy stall was being equally brave and had sold a cigarette lighter shaped like a golf ball, which only needed a new flint and some lighter fluid, and a bundle of newspapers covering the Death of George V, the Abdication of Edward VIII, and the Coronation of the new Queen. If she hadn't yet saved St. Paul's organ it was a start and she had time to adjust the angle of her knitted white beret to welcome Michael Sabini.

"So good of you to spare the time. Yes it is such fun, isn't it? Perhaps not quite as brisk as last year? Although I believe the jam is a great success, and thank goodness not so many wasps, unless the table collapses again!" Miss Hislop's laugh had a note of near hysteria that was caused not only by the memory of last year's wasps, one of which had inflated her left breast to a shape it had not known since she was 18, but by the intoxicating nearness of the curate whom she loved with a passion she only fully admitted in dreams, and in winter nights in bed even before she slept.

A curate's pay allows little for luxuries but Michael was a good boy and had been a good boy for nearly all of his twenty-two years. He would have liked to have spent a little money on Miss Hislop's stall but he had already guessed how many currants Mrs. Fowler had put in her cake, thrown unsuccessful rings at goldfish in bowls and treated children, who hadn't thanked him, to rides on swings and on Mrs. Rogers' donkey. He picked up a small piece of white pottery lying on its side near a brass ashtray. It was crudely but endearingly fashioned with three little figures sitting stiffly on a high backed settle not unlike the oldest family pews in St. Peter's. He knew the vicar had a small collection of English pottery; it would be nice to buy it for him although perhaps it wasn't quite the same as the ones he had seen on the vicarage mantle-shelf, they seemed to have more colour to them, with little branches of green leaves sticking out behind them. Perhaps, after all, this wasn't what the vicar would have liked for his collection, he may very well have seen it for himself in the morning and rejected it as too crude. Perhaps it wasn't even English, but the question was decided for him by the price, for Miss Hislop's ticket said two pounds fifty pence.

"Of course that gives only a sort of general idea of what we might sell it for, and people do so love to beat one down, we really are quite Byzantine in Lower Henworth! I rather fancy the two pounds was Mrs. Willow's suggestion she felt it might be—now what did she say? Capo di Monte, I think it was, but it just looks rather simple and jolly doesn't it? Do let's say fifty pence and I have just the right little box for it somewhere behind here." She bent over a tea chest full of pepper in which someone had brought a collection of stone hot water bottles, the dark blue of her bloomers outlined clearly against her thin cotton frock. Hers was one of the very few ladies' bottoms in the parish, Michael reflected, which had not spread to unmanageable proportions. As a bottom in itself it held no interest for him, but he wondered about her bloomers and what her re-action would be if he were to reach up with his hand at the target presented towards him and snapped the elastic hard against her leg.

"No, honestly it's very kind of you, really it is, but I think I'd better leave it. I'm sure it's quite worth two pounds fifty and we must think of the organ."

The satisfying, if somewhat disturbing, thwack of the elastic on bare flesh which mercifully had only resounded in his own head had coloured the tan on his face to an unmistakable blush, which was immediately echoed on Miss Hislop's neck and cheeks, in case he had thought she had overstepped the frontiers of Byzantium.

How very pretty and sexy he looks she thought, allowing her dream to creep out of her winter bed into the summer sunshine. In her confusion she knocked the little pottery group quite hard on the brass ashtray, which assault it survived without damage except for a small chip on the base. Noticing her embarrassment Michael decided not to mention the possible ambiguity of Miss Hislop's notice which he had originally intended to refer to tactfully. There was, however, really no way one could be tactful about it he felt, not to someone like her, poor woman; she simply would never have understood what he was trying to say. Innocence was sometimes harder to combat than vice.

Miss Hislop mentally disengaged her hand from Michael's clerical grey flannel trousers and assured him of her presence at next Sunday's Evensong.

In Flaxfield, Joan Coley the vicar's wife, stretched lunch for two to honour her husband's invitation to the architect to stay and eat with them. They sat at the table which had come to her when her sister died, thus being reunited with the dining chairs on which they had all sat as children in Folkstone and eaten well.

"I'm afraid it's a common problem," said the architect, marvelling at the number of burnt croutons Joan Coley had managed to crowd into the plate of overwatered green pea soup. "In a way you've been lucky at St. Peter's, usually if they're after lead they don't stop at two or three feet of guttering, they'll get the lot. They were disturbed obviously, but at least that leak has given us a chance to spot the real trouble."

"Real trouble," that's what her father had said when she told them she wasn't going to marry the farmer with the Bentley and the red neck. "Well now you're in real trouble my girl! This boy's a fool if ever I saw one, can't even afford to feed himself. Tells me he's had serious doubts about God and has the cheek to wear a dog collar."

"It's some of the larger timbers, dear," the dear fool said gently. "Mr. Wilson says it's dry rot and is going to cost quite a lot of money to put right."

"Oh dear, there's always something, isn't there? First the organ at Henworth and now this." She wondered if she could round off the meal after the bottled plums without referring directly to coffee. He seemed quite a nice man and even architects' wives must cut down on coffee nowadays.

"How much is a lot of money dear?"

William Coley searched for the tail of his lamb chop under the cabbage and decided regretfully that he must have eaten it without thinking. "We shall have to wait for the proper estimate of course, but Mr. Wilson thinks it could be in the region of ten thousand pounds."

Apart from Corders, the only other antique shop in Flaxfield was on the opposite side of the village, on the main road where the houses had thinned out almost losing their grip on the community which came to a full stop with the road sign that announced the end of the speed limit. It was therefore the first call for Joseph O'Shea with his horse and cart after concluding his business at the village fête at Lower Henworth. The shop had originally been two farm labourers' cottages and by sacrificing the front gardens it stood back a little from the road, newly thatched where the old roofs had been tiled, which made it look slightly top heavy. On the gravelled forecourt a cartwheel had been converted into a sign painted in black gothic script. "Old Thatched House Antiques" it said, "Adam Goodman and James Trottwood."

O'Shea loosely tethered the horse to a drainpipe and appraised the business. That thatch was new since last time and so was the sign, but the name Trottwood rang a bell—so it couldn't have changed hands. Ah now, they must have done well—grids on the windows too, sure it was fancy Spanish style iron work but grids for all that, to stop the clever fellers getting in. The geraniums in the window boxes were neatly and usefully edged with parsley.

"Is it Mr. Goodman then? Well now and haven't you done a lovely job on the whole place since I saw it last."

"I'm Mr. Trottwood, Mr. Goodman my partner is out buying."

There was something engagingly simple and nice about Jimmie Trottwood. His optimistically red wig lacked conviction but not flair. Cut defiantly in the style of the American bomber crews of the second world war, it rested like the new ginger thatch of the shop on the remnants of his own hair which was mostly pale sandy silver. The effect was startling but endearing. He suspected that sharp-eyed observers sometimes spotted the deception, at which his expression would assume a gentle melancholy like a fat cat troubled by doubt. To a select circle of intimate friends he was known as Betsey.

"Out buying! Ah wouldn't he need to do that with all the lovely things you have here. Sure now, I'm almost ashamed to show you the few sad bits I've got but now you're the expert, Mr. Trottwood, and there might just be something worth a place in a corner."

While O'Shea was humping the sack off the cart, Jimmie reflected sadly that it was always his luck to be alone in the shop when people brought things in to sell. He always missed Adam when he was away but never more than when he was expected to be knowledgeable. Adam was the brains and in all the years they had been together was frequently cross with him, but especially when he bought fakes. That dreadful old woman last year just before Christmas, telling him it had belonged to her grandmother and pointing out the gold anchor mark of Chelsea with such pride. It wasn't unknown for Adam to scream at him, but it had been an unlooked for reaction when he had shown him that sweet little porcelain duck which had been made in Paris by a man called Sampson. He would have to be very careful indeed, however handsome this young man was with the tattooed flags on his chest.

Miss Hislop, deep in her love for the curate, had looked at those same fluttering flags but, unlike Jimmie Trottwood, with no answering flutter of the heart. The thick role of rather grubby banknotes had made a more profound impression on her. "Well really. I don't know—gracious! Forty pounds! goodness! but for everything! I mean I shan't have anything left to sell." Joseph winked and started counting out the money. "And you're really supposed to bring something too," she said weakly.

There was really nothing on the cart he could have dumped on the silly old woman; when he bought he bought to sell not to give away to thin women in fields, certainly not his copper pipes or the nice bit of lead under the sacks, there would be no point in robbing Peter to pay Paul. A woman with a sticky child began turning over the brass ashtray—there was quite a bit of brass altogether. "Well now Miss, I'm a kind man and it's a good cause, I'll make it another ten and we'll have that old organ sounding out the wedding march for the glory of God and every lucky girl for miles around." He was impertinent, of course, with his crude tinker's charm and those revolting flags. You didn't say things like that in Henworth. She would refuse with dignity, let him see that they didn't need him or his greasy money. She would rather stand here in the hot sun all day. She had already warned Mrs. Willow that the eight stone hot water bottles were not the easiest things to sell in mid June, even if they were only ten pence each. She hated hot water bottles, they were an obscene comfort.

She took the money and counted it.

Well no one would fake stone hot water bottles, that was certain, thought Betsey, and if he filled them with good moist soil he could plant those nice feathery ferns in them. They would look charming and original, and he bought nearly all the bits of brass too. Adam didn't seem to mind how old brass was, tourists always liked it, especially Americans. Thirty pounds was rather a lot for the sampler but Sarah Allsop had not only worked the alphabet very prettily, she had also committed herself to Honour the Lord and Fear Death and no child of 10 in 1840 was going to sign her name in silk under that and lie about the date. "And isn't this the lovely thing now Mr. Trottwood, the three little people sitting down together and the lady in the middle with her own

dog on her lap, wouldn't that look grand in the shop or even
in the window maybe?''

The flags must have been painful for him, Jimmie
thought, and taken ages to do, too. He saw Joseph stripped
to the waist in some dim back room, perhaps it wasn't just
his chest, some boys had tattoos lower down, so that he
would have been quite naked perhaps, and the heat of the
room would have made him smell even stronger than he did
now—like a fox. He must remember to tell Adam, and
Adam would invite him to come with them for a witches
Sabbath and he could run naked with them under the moon if
it was warm enough, all flags flying, and the other designs
he could only guess at. But not if he bought a fake.

''Thank you, no, I think I'll leave that,'' he said, ''and
your horse is eating my geraniums.''

In the dining room at the vicarage, Joan Coley sat alone at
the table covered with the remains of the pinched lunch and
drank coffee. She didn't feel particularly guilty, there had
been only enough left for one cup. On the polished surface
of the table near her cup a childish pencil mark had long survived the home-made Christmas card she had drawn for her
father when she was 10. She was glad he was no longer alive
to taunt her with her poverty. On the mantel-shelf William's
little collection of pottery figures looked ashamed of their
dust in the afternoon sunshine. She would finish her coffee
and wash up, and then she would dust them for him, the
little sheep and rams, the Widow of Zarapeth with her cruse
of oil that was never empty and the barrel of meal which was
always full, and Elijah with those irritating ravens forever
offering him Ovaltine rusks. When the ravens flew over the
vicarage their gifts were less welcome and set like cement
on the windows. Ten thousand pounds; it was too much to

think about seriously. William would see someone about it. She gathered up the empty plates and the coffee cup. "Happy Christmas dear Daddy." William was a much better father to her than her own had ever been.

William, who was a practical man, had decided to waste no time and go straight to the top. He was at that moment on his knees in the fifteenth century north chantry chapel, the roof timbers of which were in no immediate danger. Such comparative safety as it afforded enabled him to concentrate his thoughts and bend his mind to the task ahead. If possible he wanted to try and avoid mentioning a miracle.

CHAPTER 3

STOCK, THOUGHT DOREEN, sooner or later I shall have to buy more stock, I can't just go on selling this stuff in the shop, and if I go out and buy in the sale-rooms to replace it, who's going to run the place? You heard terrible stories. Rupert had told her not so very long ago about a widow just outside Ipswich who had engaged a young man, highly educated with pink cheeks, he had been quite perfect, beautifully spoken and anxious to learn everything about the antique business and after nine months he had, and disappeared with every penny in the bank and most of the stock while she was visiting her mother in Glasgow. Thank God, Rupert had said, that they only had to rely on each other, complete trust was the strongest asset any business could have. Well now he was gone. Next Tuesday they would bring him from the undertakers in Rutley and he would be buried in the churchyard of St. Peter's, where they had attended morning service almost every Sunday because some of their best customers had done the same. It was a good place for contacts, perhaps lunch with old clients afterwards to admire their collections and to remind them of past bargains and future hopes; or a drink in the Bull to develop new prospects. Sometimes they had opened the shop for them on Sunday afternoons. She felt cheated.

"Now as I understand it Lord," said the vicar, who saw no reason why Omniscience should not be aided by an up-to-date report, "the main trouble appears to be in some of the larger beams over the nave—not all of them, it seems, but I'm afraid that with the cost of labour and inflation the estimate might come as rather a shock to you."

Doreen's knowledge of antiques was sketchy but she knew more than Jimmie Trottwood. As far as she could remember she had never seen a piece of pottery quite like it but some instinct told her that it was good—very good. Mentally she saw Rupert's head incline appreciatively to the left.

The man was lolling in a newly covered button-back Victorian chair, but since it had a protective sheet of thick clear plastic over it, she was content to let him sit there until she could find out what he wanted for it. He had slipped forward on the shiny transparent cover so that his trousers were stretched tight over his thighs and his shirt bulged open to reveal the Irish Tricolour and the Union Jack entwined above the legend *Brothers unto Death*. It had originally and optimistically proclaimed the single word *Brothers,* the hopeful design of a lady tattooist in Liverpool much influenced by the Women's Peace Movement in Belfast. The design had not sold well and she had resented making the addition, only acceding to Joseph's request when he had given her a graphic description of his acute embarrassment in a Dublin pub, an encounter not unmingled with moments of real danger.

If she went on staring at the piece of pottery on the table between them he would think she was too interested in it and ask more. If she looked at him it might seem to suggest an interest in him that she felt but had no intention of revealing. It was pleasant to know that she could still feel like that, the fire that Rupert had fanned so energetically and gymnastically through the years had never done more than glow resentfully, until she had come to believe that she was probably frigid and that those happy leaping flames had disappeared with the boys on the Welsh mountains of her youth.

"Yes, it's quite pleasant but I'm afraid it's a little late for us, we have a very strict dateline you know, our customers expect it and trust us."

"They would, they would surely, with all the little labels with the dates and the grand old church just across the road."

"My husband is very particular."

"A man of taste, you can see that." He lifted his arms cupping his hands behind his neck so that his shirt closed modestly across his chest but revealed the more detailed shape of his body beneath the now straining cloth of the trousers, which display he made no attempt to conceal.

A sudden flame, longer and hotter than the rest, flicked unexpectedly and deliciously through the flimsy and inadequate defence of her summer knickers. "Of course, we do have customers for later things. It depends what you want for it."

Still with his hands behind his head he stretched so that his body made a stiff straight line from his heels to his neck. "Well now," he said, carefully addressing the old damp patch on the ceiling, "with you having to be so careful an' that, I could wait maybe and see what—Mr. Corder is it? What Mr. Corder would offer for it."

She turned the pottery over but there was no mark of any kind underneath. "He won't be back for some time; you'd better say."

Rising, he came and stood behind her chair looking over her head as she held the piece in her hands, steadying them on the table top. "That's a saucy feller," he said. "The one on the right with his hand resting on the lady's breast like that. And a risk too, she could slap his face or the pug might go for him, they can be very snappy, pugs."

Doreen had no pug to defend her and neither did she slap his face. She did move quickly to the door, but only to lock it and display the notice she reserved for less urgent calls of nature. "Stock-taking," it said, "Back Later."

In her semi-detached house, near a respectable part of the main railway line in Cardiff, her mother surveyed her legs with satisfaction. Now encased in new flesh-coloured elastic stockings they gave her a sense of security she had not felt since the distant days of her competition ball-room dancing. They would never again get her to the semi-finals in the Latin American section but, with luck, they ought to get her as far as Flaxfield, for her son-in-law's funeral. The whole business had been a great shock to her. One minute Doreen had been nicely settled and looking forward to Marbella again in September, and then overnight a widow, with nothing decent to wear for the funeral.

Mrs. Thomas had neither liked or disliked Rupert Corder, but when they had all first met on that holiday in Weston-Super-Mare and he had shown an interest in Doreen she had seen a security and stability for her daughter that she felt might not come again. What disturbed her now was not knowing. She didn't know how much money there was, and she didn't know whether Doreen would be able to manage on her own, and if she couldn't manage on her own Mrs. Thomas felt she should be in a position to invigilate any future plans her daughter might even now be contemplating. Doreen's plans she reflected had always needed careful watching. Flighty, that's what she was, flighty, given to making hasty decisions not always wise. If it hadn't been for her, Doreen might well have spent the last fifteen years in the Wrens or married to one of those dreadful valley boys who used to call for her on motor bikes and take her up to the mountains to pick wimberries. Rupert, twenty years her senior, had been the perfect cure for all that, providing her with security and an accent that sounded English in Cardiff and Welsh in Flaxfield. Thank God the inquest and the post mortem had delayed the funeral, for it had become quite obvious to her when chatting tactfully with Doreen on the phone that the funeral arrangements, if left to her, could be a travesty unworthy of the name of Thomas. She decided not to risk the skills or taste of an English florist, she would get the wreath made properly in Cardiff and take it with her, and the ham, however much Doreen might protest that people didn't eat ham at English funerals. It might just be true but was more likely an excuse, Doreen could be lazy sometimes unless stirred. Flighty and lazy; what a blessing her legs were better, it would be a shambles without her.

"Well, there it is Lord, I'll let you have the estimate of course as soon as it comes in and you must decide. I've always found it difficult, as you know, asking for help with restorations, we do what we can ourselves, the organ at Henworth and so on, but I rather fancy this is going to be a bit beyond us. Frankly, I don't honestly see how you could consider it when you must need so much money for real trouble, like Ireland, and famines with children hungry, but I tell myself I mustn't try and do your job but only your will. Anyway, thank you Lord, I know you'll do what you can. We're a fairly ordinary lot round here as you know, nothing special, but without boasting I think we get above average numbers—you may have noticed last Sunday's evensong perhaps?"

It was a measure of the vicar's niceness that naïvety that he never mentioned that he was quite often hungry himself and that the beauty of St. Peter's was rivalled by the beauty of Michael Sabini who had a strong local fan club.

Doreen may have run true to her mother's estimation of her character, it was certainly a hasty decision she made when she had felt Joseph's hand slide down over her shoulder but it was one she had no cause to regret. She was not frigid. That idea disappeared when she lay on the bed and watched him undress deliberately and without hurrying. She clasped the union of Ireland and England to her more fiercely than Gladstone at the height of his dream and, as if calling upon her mother to witness that she was truly not lazy, she fanned the flames until it seemed they must both be consumed in fire and frenzy. Although Doreen herself was not in a position to see it, Jimmie Trottwood had been perfectly correct in his speculations. The tattooist's art was not confined to Joseph's chest. On the cheeks of Joseph's bottom two gaudy tropical butterflies writhed and twisted in a desperate effort to escape the flames, leaping and turning faster and faster until it seemed they must surely succeed and, tearing free, flutter into the cool air through the bedroom window, high over the house and the road, over the unsafe roof at St. Peter's and into the calm and peace of the sun setting quietly and respectably over Flaxfield.

All through the remainder of that long hot afternoon and evening the little white pottery group lay on the table where Doreen had left it. From time to time people paused and looked into the locked shop, browsers baulked of free entertainment, a few prospective customers who might or might not return another day, two local residents to sympathize and console her in her grief. In the late twilight they had all gone, even though some had looked harder and longer than others. The butterflies, exhausted by their unexpected long flight, came to rest gratefully and were decently and modestly covered as he sat on the edge of the bed to put on his shoes. Doreen very much wanted to tell him there was no hurry, but having begun the evening with Rupert alive there seemed no way she could explain. Perhaps it was best after all, she wouldn't have to bother with food but have a sandwich and watch News at Ten.

Joseph hoped he could get away before the pub shut: beer for himself and water for his horse. In many ways he was a sensitive man.

''Wouldn't it be best,'' he said, gingerly pushing his shirt down into his trousers, ''to go quiet out the back and not ruffle the street?''

Doreen, surprised and touched by such unexpected thoughtfulness, agreed gratefully that it would. Alone, she stood in the gloom of the shop in her dressing gown only long enough to put the pottery group away in Rupert's cupboard before climbing rather stiffly back up the stairs. She wouldn't bother with a sandwich. Tomorrow she must look at some of Rupert's books on pottery. Perhaps it was quite worthless but then she hadn't paid any money for it so it was a bargain whichever way you looked at it. Joseph, drinking his third pint outside the Bull watched affectionately as his horse finished a bucket of water, they were both glad to see each other. It was almost past drinking-up time and they had the forecourt to themselves.

"Sometimes Katie," confided Joseph, "you can do well with a nice bit of lead or an old barometer, but I'll tell you my girl that was the best bloody bargain I've ever had, and isn't that the truth?"

In the bar of the Connaught Hotel in Mount Street, London where there was no drinking-up time for residents, Gaylord W. Whitman, Jnr. sipped a large tumbler of Scotch whisky and Malvern water with no ice and looked at the photograph with fierce concentration, as if willing it to become clearer and more explicit. It was difficult to say why he should look American. Almost everything he wore he had bought in London, including his suit, his tailored shirt, and his shoes, hand-lasted in fine calf. If it had been October and not June he would have worn a bowler hat which he would not have called a Derby and carried a rolled umbrella which would not have shamed a Guards officer. He adored England and contrived to give the impression, without actually saying so, that he bitterly resented the loss of the Empire. Yet his features and trim figure marked him unmistakably as a nice rich middle-aged American college boy, with a confident sun tan and a tie so nearly right it was desperately wrong.

"Goddam it Eddie, how the hell can I tell from this?"

"I know it's bad but it's the best I could get. If it had been in the window you'd see what I mean but that table must have been at least ten feet away. It's the best I could get with a Polaroid."

Eddie Cabert was a runner, he spent nearly all his time on a Japanese motor bike scouring remote corners of the country for antiques. When he couldn't buy, he photographed. He knew what half the world wanted, and with single minded industry he sometimes found it in the other half. With his jeans and his tee shirt and leather jacket he aimed for the open, honest look of an American college boy, but his pale face and small anxious eyes, his shrewd knowledge and lack of confidence placed him firmly in the backstreet antique markets of London and limited him to the occasional successful bid in Sotheby's Belgravia.

Gaylord Whitman looked wistfully at the jumbled objects in the photograph just in case he had missed some faint clue as to where this treasure shop might be located, and failed.

"And it was closed, huh?"

"For stock-taking it said."

"You saw it, d'you think it's right?"

"I think it could be, I'll know if I can see it close."

"Jesus! What the hell can they ask for a thing like that?"

"It depends, there's some nice things there, you can see that it's not junky. They must know what it's worth—or what they think it's worth, but for you it could still be a bargain."

In the dining room, Mrs. Whitman, after a baffling encounter with Harold Pinter in the theatre, would be recovering in the air-conditioned luxury and mentally savouring one of the best menus in Europe. To keep her waiting another five minutes might ruin the evening for both of them.

"O.K. Eddie," he said, "get it. I'll pay. You'd better eat before you go. Is it far?"

It was a question Eddie had no intention of answering, he had expected Whitman to do his level best to trap him into giving away some clue. He knew perfectly well that if the American could deal direct with the shop Eddie Cabert would be fobbed off with a commission fee and that, however generous, would be nothing like the profit Eddie had every intention of making if he could.

"They won't let me eat here, dressed like this," he said.

"I guess you're right. Wait, I'll have them make up some sandwiches for you. Have another beer."

When he left the bar Whitman made a telephone call before ordering the sandwiches.

When Eddie had gone, clutching the food under the disapproving eye of the barman, the American found that his hands were shaking with frustrated excitement. The last thing he wanted was food but he took a tranquillizer and some indigestion tablets. Then he joined his wife in the dining room; her eyes glittered ominously in a face raddled by central heating and rejuvenating cream.

"Gee, honey, I'm sorry," he said.

CHAPTER 4

MRS. THOMAS HAD done her best for Doreen but there was
no doubt that English funerals were sad affairs with no joy in
them. Without her, she reflected, it would have been very
flat indeed. Doreen had even wanted to keep the shop open
in the few days left before the Interment, instead of having
every blind and curtain closed to the world to show proper
grief and to keep the gaze of the vulgar away from the preparations of the funeral feast, poor thing though it would be by
any civilized standards. Doreen hadn't even known that
there were roller blinds which could be pulled down to cover
the shop windows. A little shabby, perhaps, with one or two
cracks and holes and one of them had a worn catch and an
unnerving tendency to fly up with a noise like a sonic boom.
Rupert's coffin, decently delivered by the undertakers, now
lay supported by a sixteenth century oak chest in the centre
of the shop, thus being available for easy access to the road
for its penultimate journey in the morning, and giving Mrs.
Thomas plenty of room to make arrangements for the mod-

est gathering she had planned to follow the service at St. Peter's. Sadly, she had been forced to agree with Doreen, that it seemed hardly necessary to bring the hearse all the way back from Rutley in the morning merely to cross the road and she had agreed to accept six bearers instead. She suspected that Doreen had been motivated by meanness judging by the way she had complained already about the cost of the food and the expense of the service and burial. "There's a notice in the church, Mam, I wrote it down. 'Service in church before burial, burial of body in churchyard immediately following the service in church of the same parish' comes to thirteen pounds, that's five to the Vicar and eight to the parochial church council. That's quite a lot, you know, Mam, and God knows what the bill from the undertaker will be."

Flighty, lazy and mean, that's what she was, thank God her poor Dada had never lived to see it, to be shamed by seeing his daughter wearing the same clothes she'd worn at his own funeral. She thought with pride of his lovely coffin with the top quality handles and the two extra cars to carry the flowers alone, while poor Rupert would cross the road to eternity with barely enough flowers to hide the pitiful plainness of what she suspected was the very cheapest box Doreen could find. A sorry way to go on the most important day of his life. At least she'd had enough sense to insist on bringing the ham but she doubted if she would get much help with the sandwiches.

At the other end of the village Jimmie Trottwood was doing his best to disperse the remains of the unhappy gloom which had descended upon Old Thatched House ever since he had proudly displayed the things he had bought from Joseph O'Shea. For once it wasn't that he had bought anything which had displeased Adam but rather one of the things which Jimmie had, equally proudly, told him he had turned down. At first sight Adam Goodman would have passed for an ex-army officer or a successful businessman and he had been neither of these. His closest acquaintance with the army was his two year period as a National serviceman during which he had briefly risen to the rank of corporal before being granted an honourable discharge at the end of it. His business career had been less honourable for he was a compulsive liar and, lacking that essential quality of a good memory, successive employers had sacked him with depressing regularity through the years. To bolster his bruised ego, each sacking left him with a thicker veneer of military respectability, wearing quiet well-tailored suits which he had never paid for, rising through the ranks until when he first met Jimmie informally in a public lavatory in the Fulham Road, he was a well set up Major of thirty with a smart moustache, a good working knowledge of antiques, a fondness for gambling and a grand manner which had swept Betsey Trottwood off his feet and what little money he had into Adam's bank account. Curiously it was a reasonable success. Betsey for all his silliness, was the shrewder of the two; he was not only lovable but he had a fund of love to give in return and he was generous with it. His love didn't change Adam's character but modified it, letting him bask in reflected popularity so that people who didn't know him well came to think him as honest as his partner. Betsey with no misgivings left his safe job in Peter Jones and allowed Adam to buy junk antiques which they sold successfully from a stall in Portabello market. When Betsey's mother died they bought and converted the little cottages in Flaxfield where Betsey dressed the windows to his heart's content and talked Adam out of becoming a colonel. They were accepted by the village as much as any stranger is ever accepted and since Betsey was as full of good deeds as any nineteenth century lady of the manor they were assumed to be equally kind. Both of them were regular attendants at St. Peter's: Betsey because he was naturally a paid up member of the Michael Sabini fan club and willingly paid his dues into the collecting box every time Michael was billed to appear, and Adam because church was a good background for an army major and it helped him to keep an eye on the Corders' clients.

One of Michael's most interesting, although misinformed, sermons had been a solemn warning on the dangers and false attractions for the young of dabbling in the occult. One of the Sunday papers had been carrying a highly sensational account of the witches' covens cavorting naked under a full moon through the pastures of East Anglia. "Boys and girls," said Michael warming to his theme, "in the full flower and beauty of their youth seduced by false gods from the path of true righteousness and Christian virtue." The sermon had made a deep impression on Betsey. Although no longer in the full flower and beauty of his youth he would have dearly loved to have run naked through the fields and woods with those who were. He had no intention of being seduced from the path of true righteousness (especially if Michael Sabini was prepared to lead the way) but the thought of perhaps being able to lead some of the naked sinners back to the path was an excuse to soothe away any qualms of conscience. Just to see them, he thought wistfully, would be nice. He had followed all the articles in the Sunday paper but they were disappointingly vague when it came to pinpointing the exact fields and woods but, as he explained to Adam, they would naturally have to vary their meeting places for fear of discovery. When the delightful series finished and no echoing details ever appeared in the

East Anglian Daily News, Betsey read everything on witch-craft from the county library until he became quite knowl-edgeable. His enthusiasm even broke through Adam's military defences and scepticism and when the moon was full they had taken to abandoning their local pub in Flaxfield and could be seen walking through the long lanes over to the Henworth Arms peering hopefully over the hedgerows across the meadows, and willing the rich velvet shadow at the edge of the woods to disgorge the youth of East Anglia disporting itself with naked abandon and enthusiasm. So far they had seen nothing.

But tonight, Betsey sensed, was not the time to pursue his new enthusiasm. Adam must be wooed into a happier mood, even a blazing row would have been better than the cold po-liteness Adam almost always used as a barrier when he was displeased. He hoped it wouldn't come to that but if so he was perfectly prepared to suffer it to clear the air. It would be no worse than having a tooth out, when relief and peace would follow the pain. The trouble was, neither of them was quite sure which tooth was aching. It needn't of course come to a row at all, sometimes Adam's mood would unaccount-ably disappear, the gloom would disperse, the sun would shine down on the thatch and the threatened storm never de-velop. In the hope that this might happen Betsey had made a special effort with the supper, preparing a roast chicken and salad according to the recipe guaranteed to be non-fattening. He himself had long ago abandoned the fight against his spreading waistline but if Adam still aimed at a trim military figure he should be helped with all the skill at Betsey's com-mand, which was why *Escoffier's Guide to Modern Cook-ery* had been replaced by *Cuisine Minceur* on the kitchen shelf.

While Adam sat waiting for supper, unsuitably squeezed

into artificially faded blue jeans, Betsey flopped hopefully between kitchen and dining alcove more honestly and practically clad in a plastic pinny proclaiming the virtues of Guinness. Ignoring his own advertisement he gave Adam a glass of dry sherry and opened one of the last good bottles of white Loire wine, tentatively humming a few catchy bars from *Patience*.

In the dining room of the Connaught the richest and creamiest of Escoffier's menus had settled uneasily at the pit of Gaylord Whitman's stomach. Expecting to be welcomed with love and gratitude it had encountered a suspicious barrier of magnesium hydroxide and activated methylpolysiloxane. Resolving itself into a tight knot of resentment it remained unloved and largely undigested, sending up small distress signals of peppermint scented poison gas into the already unhappy atmosphere of the table above.

"I don't see why it has to be so important for me to go with you."

"Because I want you to, this was supposed to be my trip, remember? Theatre and opera."

"Well we've done that."

"Sure and dragged round crummy antique shops every day so that you can sleep through every goddam show we've been to."

"Honey, I have to be here tomorrow, this may be the rarest and most important piece I'll ever find for the collection. I may never get the chance again. If you don't want to go on your own I'll have the London office here fix someone to take you, anyway for Chrissake what's so special about Glyndbourne?"

"Because you told me, on a lousy dried up lawn in South Hampton that Glyndbourne had the greenest lawns in the world, that it was the soul of English opera. Magic, you said. Air like champagne, you said. We have four houses with beautiful cool air and you keep dragging me halfway across the world to breathe hot dust all day and sit in theatres where they light a fire under your ass in midsummer so that you can buy your lousy bits of pottery and snore even through the intermission.''

The tables at the Connaught are not crowded and her silent tears slipped unnoticed over the sealed surface of her face on to her unfinished Charlotte a L'Arlequine.

Mrs. Thomas ran a thin testing knife into the thickest part of the ham she had brought with her from Cardiff which was now simmering gently in a large preserving pan she had had to borrow from Joan Coley, Doreen's kitchen being ill-equipped to deal with funeral feasts. As the Vicar's wife, Joan was not accustomed to expect visitors tapping unannounced at her kitchen door. For Doreen's mother it was a perfectly normal procedure among neighbours. The borrowing had taken less time than Mrs. Thomas had expected but longer than either the Vicar or his wife could have anticipated. When, after nearly an hour, he had come diplomatically to see how the baked beans and poached eggs were progressing for his overdue supper he found the two ladies chatting happily and the kitchen air innocent of burnt toast.

''Oh William, I *am* sorry, I'm afraid we've been talking and quite forgotten the time. Mrs. Thomas has very kindly asked us over for some food after the funeral; apparently it's quite usual in Wales, isn't that interesting?''

''Really? How very kind, however I think perhaps . . .''

''Mrs. Thomas came to borrow something to cook the ham in, Mrs. Corder has nothing big enough.''

William looked at the large pan on the kitchen table

thoughtfully, hunger and imagination magically filling it with pink poetry, like a colour plate in *Mrs. Beeton*. The economic squeeze had meant sacrifices for everyone; William neither had private means nor did his wife have a separate income. Parishioners who in the past had been generous with the occasional gift of meat could now barely afford it for themselves. Ham he had come to think of as paper-thin slices in sandwiches—not as something to be carved nobly from the bone.

"We shall be delighted," he said, "only . . ." His wife's face expressed anxiety tinged with desperation. "Only what, William?" she said, disappointment sharpening her voice more than she had intended.

"Oh my dear, of course you must go," William said quickly, years of marriage translating her thoughts accurately for him, "but I'm afraid I promised Michael—my fine young curate, you know, Mrs. Thomas—that I would manage a working lunch with him, a sandwich and a glass of beer perhaps."

"Can't he come too?" demanded Mrs. Thomas, "plenty for all, the more the merrier."

When the clanking of the huge preserving pan had faded away William sat and watched his wife prepare their modest supper. He would, he thought, be able to keep an eye on the toast for her so that she could concentrate on the beans and poached eggs.

"Nice of her to ask Michael, wasn't it?" he said.

She smiled at him fondly. "Yes wasn't it—she's a nice woman, a bit odd but I liked her. I couldn't help it, she kept making me laugh, she's quite different from Flaxfield. She showed me her legs, says she can still feel quite sexy when they're not playing her up."

"She didn't!"

"She did, I swear, I couldn't help laughing. More honest than some of our old biddies anyway. Here we are, I'm afraid the eggs have broken a bit."

Betsey's meal had gone very well indeed, leaving Adam considerably brighter. The gloom had lifted perceptively making it a positive pleasure for him to wash up while Adam sat reading. For all his basic nastiness he loved Betsey and was well aware that without him he would never have what they now shared. He was maddening, of course, infuriating even, the way he forgot things. While the chicken was cooking he had taken him slowly through some of the illustrations in the books on English pottery to see if he could recognize anything similar to the piece he had refused to buy from Joseph O'Shea, but with no success. O'Shea was ignorant but he had a basic instinct and some of the things he had brought them in the past they had sold extremely well. But fancy not even being able to describe something he had seen so recently, just because the horse had been nibbling his bloody geraniums, serve him right for planting parsley with them. He'd remembered that stupid tattoo all right, silly cat. Oh well, perhaps it hadn't been anything special after all—"Just a little thingy" as Betsey had called it. Too late now anyway, best forget it.

In the kitchen Betsey switched off the radio, removed his pinny and adjusted his crew cut before preparing for a relaxed and happier evening. They might walk over to Henworth, it wasn't quite a full moon, but you never knew. "Oh! Look!" he leaned over Adam's chair from behind and pointed a plump finger at a photograph of a Pew Group without reading the caption. "Now that's *very* like it—oh yes! almost exactly. What is it love?"

* * *

Mrs. Thomas withdrew the testing knife and sniffed at it delicately. Pongs a bit, she thought. P'raps I should've cooked it in Cardiff.

CHAPTER 5

So far, thought Mrs. Thomas at the graveside, every-thing had gone reasonably well. It wasn't to be compared with the best that she had been used to but by hard work and application to her duty she felt that she had saved the occasion from complete dullness and mediocrity. It had to be said that the church itself was a more impressive setting than the more austere Welsh chapels which had formed the background for the funerals of the many friends and neighbours she had enjoyed through the years—culminating in the supreme effort she had made for her own husband who had succumbed prematurely to a surfeit of nagging and fried bread.

The policeman had held up the traffic for the undertaker's six bearers to carry Rupert across the road, although he had not worn white gloves nor saluted, and there had been a distressing lack of interest on the part of Flaxfield shoppers, none of whom had removed their hats or shown any real enthusiasm. Things had improved at the entrance to the churchyard of St. Peter's where the Vicar and his curate had awaited them at the lych-gate. The service itself had been a sad business enlivened only by the hymns which she had chosen herself and bullied Doreen into demanding.

"Death has been here, and borne away
A scholar from our side.
We cannot tell who next may fall
Beneath Thy chastening rod;
One must be first, but let us all
Prepare to meet our God."

Since she had had the foresight to bring the music with her all opposition had crumbled. Although she had considered the attendance poor, in fact by Flaxfield standards Rupert had done quite well, with a sprinkling of antique collectors, the landlord and barmaid from The Bull, together with a few regulars who had cause to be grateful for Rupert's generosity towards closing time and who had heard rumours of the impressive wine and spirit order Mrs. Thomas had placed for the feast to come. Most of the faces were known to Doreen but there were some she couldn't place. She was still walking rather gingerly after her battle with the butterflies and, more than a little appalled by the amount her mother was spending, hoped that Psalm 39 was prophetic when it informed her that Rupert may have been heaping up riches even if it expressed doubts as to who was going to gather them.

Now at the graveside, she tried not to look at her mother's hat with the dyed black straw giving off a curious iridescence and a faint but penetrating scent like stale turnips. Looking around her at the faces surrounding the open grave she noted that there was no sign of anyone who could be remotely described as Gentry—just Trade and small collectors and hangers-on from the pub. She felt a mild sense of anger and resentment, it was a rotten way to treat her husband after the way he had helped many of them to build up their stupid collections, sometimes bidding for them at important auctions, occasionally being rewarded with a sherry but never asked for meals. Poor Rupert, he was well rid of them, better without them.

"He cometh up, and is cut down, like a flower."

The Old Thatched House Antiques stood together a little apart from the others. Adam because he was sincerely ashamed of himself and didn't feel like talking to anyone, and Betsey because he hoped that under its thick layer of Max Factor Pancake his black eye might escape notice. He had endured scorn and belittlement through the years, and had survived Adam's occasional fits of screaming and abuse but he had never before been physically attacked. Even now as they stood together in the presence of death and that ghastly wreath Mrs. Corder's mother was clutching he was not at all certain what he really felt about it all. Bewilderment certainly, amazement even, that had been his first reaction, seeing the white fury on Adam's face even before his fist had sent him reeling into a pyramid of stone hot water bottles filled with damp soil and baby ferns. Even before he had been able to find his wig Adam had thrust the book under his nose and, in a quiet deliberate voice that sounded more awful than any scream, read what the book said about Pew Groups.

The rarest and most desirable examples of the English potters' art of the early eighteenth century. Only some twenty or so pieces of these enchanting naïve groups are known to exist. Nearly all of them are to be found in the great museum collections of the world. Sometimes attributed to Aaron Wood their exact origin is of little consequence. Should any new examples ever appear they would undoubtedly be worth a King's ransom.

Before this terrible passage had finished Betsey had found his wig under a little pile of John Innes potting compost and was unwisely trying to adjust it to regain some semblance of dignity in a world that seemed about to end there and then on the floor of the dining alcove. In this manoeuvre he was frustrated by Adam who read the last two lines so that each word was separated and emphasized with great shoves on his shoulder until the words "King's ransom" sent the wig flying to the floor again. And there, this time, he left it, nor did he attempt to get up. Adam rose and tossed the book down at him before crossing to sit in a chair, glaring at him in silence. For nearly three minutes he sat looking at Betsey who still lay among the ruins of his ingeniously potted ferns not raising his tear-filled eyes and too shattered and miserable even to blow his nose. A wave of self-revulsion and regret brought Adam back to him to help him to his feet and sit him in a chair. Then he went back for the wig shaking most of the earth from it and helping to put it straight.

Over the top of the handkerchief Betsey's one operative eye fixed Adam bravely. "You're a rotten bastard."

"I know, I'm sorry—truly."

Betsey tried, only partially successfully, to focus on his reflection in a reproduction looking-glass above the sideboard. "You forgot to get the washing-up liquid," he said, "I hate running out."

"We can buy some tomorrow after the funeral."

* * *

The weather, which had started bright and sunny had now improved, Mrs. Thomas noted with satisfaction, the sky becoming grey and overcast and altogether more appropriate for the occasion. She would have liked a little light drizzle, not a drenching downpour, people had been known to desert open gravesides even before the Interment in really heavy rain, but a scattering of gleaming black umbrellas would have been nice to calm down the jollity of June. Although she had coerced Doreen into inviting as many people as she could think of she still had an uneasy feeling that she had catered for far more guests than would actually appear. The English were a funny lot, she had had a distinct impression that the invitations had taken many of them by surprise. The thought that some might not even appear in spite of their assurances was almost spoiling the whole ceremony for her, but she told herself not to be morbid. At least with no rain falling, she would be able to whip round the graveside afterwards confirming acceptances from faces she remembered and rounding up any potential guests from the periphery like a border collie at a sheepdog trial.

From the kitchen window of the vicarage Joan Coley watched the group gathered round the open grave. Funerals were so much a part of William's stock in trade that she seldom even noticed them. That funny little Mrs. Thomas with her invitation to food and drinks afterwards caused her to reconsider her attitude in this instance. In the end she had decided to postpone her shopping until later in the afternoon and compromise out of courtesy by attending the church service and discreetly absenting herself from the churchyard. The hymn tunes had seemed jollier than the ones she was accustomed to hearing, and louder, and quicker in tempo, even though William had asked her to warn Mr. Routledge the organist to ignore all passages marked "fortissimo" and that if he should be so foolhardy as to obey the injunction fortissimo on,

"Thy awful wrath send down"

they all might very well join Mr. Corder in a common grave.

By skipping the churchyard bit she could catch up on a few of the morning's chores and still keep an eye on them across the gravestones so that she could join them when it was over. William, she thought, really looked quite impressive conducting the service in dumbshow. With firm mouth and chin and only the hair above his ears beginning to look grey, almost white, quite like a real vicar. What an odd bouncy little woman that Mrs. Thomas was, happily devouring William's every word and gesture, perhaps her legs weren't playing her up too badly today and she fancied him. She levered up a thin carpet of baked beans from the bottom of the saucepan which experience had long since taught her was best left soaking overnight. She still fancied William herself and, bless him, he was not always unresponsive but overwork and undernourishment had made their occasional essays more an expression of affection and kindness than in the rousing early days when she had felt deliciously unsafe even in the vestry. The happy memories receded rapidly as she noticed with mild dismay that Bunter, the black and white vicarage tom cat, was sitting tidily on a flat gravestone as near as he could get to the proceedings and was following the service with interest. In some ways he was a cat of morbid pursuits and seldom missed a burial if he could help it. William was far too indulgent with him, she thought. She unblocked the sink with a long piece of metal coat hanger.

"Oh Holy and most merciful Saviour deliver us not unto
the bitter pains of eternal death."

It was very kind of them, William thought, to ask him and
Joan to the party across the road after the service. Well, perhaps party was hardly the right word but kind just the same.
A curious people, the Welsh. He had intended to leave the
question of the Pew Group until a decent interval of time had
elapsed but that would call for the most heroic restraint.
Suppose she sold it before he could broach the subject?
To some casual enquirer perhaps? and even—his hands
clutched his prayer book in real distress—without realizing
its true rarity and value? That he had seen it displayed
clearly in the shop while she had been stock-taking he had
no doubt. He had gazed longingly at the ones in the
Fitzwilliam Museum in Cambridge too often for there to be
any mistake. How could she have come by something as
wonderful as that in Flaxfield? And, more important, was
there some chance that he might come to own it for himself?
He would see that she made a handsome profit, of course.
What was he thinking such nonsense for? How could he
know what she had given for it? It may even have been
something Corder himself had bought and kept in a cupboard against hard times, in which case she would surely
know its true value. On the other hand . . . perhaps if he offered her his entire collection for just that one piece? She
might do very well out of those, some of them were really
very nice examples and the Widow of Zarapeth was almost
perfect.

"Thou knowest, Lord, the secrets of our hearts"

There was just a chance, thought Adam, that O'Shea

could have sold it to Doreen Corder; he was not likely to leave the village without trying the only other antique shop. Unless the silly bitch had been closed, in which case God alone knew where it was now. Somehow he must get hold of Doreen and question her discreetly. News of the funeral feast was common gossip in the pub with Doreen's mother ordering on a scale they usually only expected at Christmas. Bloody barbarians the Welsh. If he had spent more time in the Bull recently instead of ruining his best shoes in wet grass looking for nonexistent naked witches they would probably have been invited themselves. He would make himself as pleasant and solicitous as he could after the service and with luck they would still be asked.

Doreen was very near to tears. So far she had borne up bravely comforting herself with the thought of her new found freedom lying ahead of her. The presence of her mother with her chatter and questions and endless preparations had only allowed her brief moments to consider her situation, and she had retired behind a mask of quiet acceptance which could be mistaken for grief, but which really disguised something very close to panic. Not panic for fear of retribution, for her limited sense of responsibility had firmly labelled Rupert's death as an accident, the result of a lighthearted tomboy jest that had gone tragically awry and about which it was best not to think, much less allot any blame herself. Her panic was for her future stretching unfettered but horribly uncertain before her without the support and knowledge of the man who had bored her for the last fifteen years and kept her in comfort and modest luxury. It didn't seem possible that he was really in that coffin which even now was being lowered into the grave on a June morning not fifty yards from his shop while the Eastern Counties bus passed by on its way to Ipswich.

Betsey sensed Doreen's distress, and the frightened tears behind her eyes which threatened to flow at any moment, were anticipated by his own which ran effortlessly over the patch of make-up under his black eye, making it look like a victoria plum nibbled by wasps. He longed to go over and put his arm around her for comfort. He had never known her very well but she had always been very nice to him when they had sometimes met in the shops and she had given him a recipe for paella which had been a great success. Rupert he had found distant and a little frightening.

"We therefore commit this body to the ground."

Mrs. Thomas, who had been reluctant to relinquish her wreath and place it with the other miserable tokens which apparently passed for floral tributes, now braced herself. Throughout the ceremony in the churchyard she had preferred to hold it propped up in front of her, in which position it had served the dual purpose of shaming the assembled mourners with its glories of missed white lilies and the initials RC picked out in red carnations, and of partially hiding the bright flesh-pink of her elastic stockings gleaming through the black of her nylons. With a shiver of anticipatory excitement she now placed it reverently on the gravel path in front of her and prepared to luxuriate in the public comfort of her daughter.

The sun which had been threatening to dispel the pleasant atmosphere of gloom now retreated behind a pall of grey cloud. Miss Hislop, having ascertained that the curate was to be present, at last managed to push in front of the curious little man clad in black leather and holding a motor cycle crash helmet the better to observe her hero.

On the north side of the cemetery, in the rutted lane that

ran down a gentle slope to join the main road, Joseph O'Shea's horse tentatively breathed on the yew hedge and wisely decided against it. Joseph sat on the box of the cart, not so far away across the churchyard that he could not clearly distinguish the faces around the open grave.

Ten miles to the west, Gaylord W. Whitman Jnr. sat in a chauffeur-driven Rolls Royce waiting for a small herd of incontinent Fresian cows, oblivious to the tortures of a dedicated collector, to cross the road in disarray.

Bunter, seeing that the best of the drama was over, allowed his senses, more firmly attuned than the rest of the mourners, to savour the various messages that drifted past his nose as he sat on the flat tombstone. The sad echo of burnt baked beans was joined on the breeze by the persistent odour of dry rot from the open door of the church. They mingled with the curious scent of the dyed straw hat and the smell of lilies past their best. It was not pleasant and held little promise, but from across the road in the unlikely direction of the antique shop, came faint but happy signals which encouraged further investigation.

Joan Coley watched him jump down unhurriedly and stretch, before casually cocking his tail with experienced accuracy and spraying Mrs. Thomas's wreath with a stink so powerful that it effectively smothered all grief and made William lose his place in the Collect. The carpet of burnt baked beans darted through her fingers and slipped into the lower depths to block the sink again. She left it to work out its own salvation and prepared to join the others.

As Mrs. Thomas was herding the last of the stragglers into a compact knot near the lych-gate, Joseph still sat on the box seat of the cart with a firm grip on the reins. Katie would have very much liked to move on down the lane in search of something more appetizing than yew, but Joseph, whose senses were if anything even more finely attuned than Bunter's, had a curious feeling that perhaps the drama had only just begun.

CHAPTER 6

ON THE MORNING of Rupert's funeral, Detective Inspector John Webber waited for Dr. Maguire to return to his surgery. The empty waiting room, like the house itself, was well proportioned with pleasant pale green walls and fresh white paint round the french windows which opened on to a neglected lawn. The door to the doctor's surgery was open and, like the waiting room, it confirmed his taste for solid Victorian furniture. Nothing matched but it looked comfortable and reassuring. The surgery in Webber's brief professional survey suggested a man of about sixty, perhaps a bachelor but more likely a widower. The desk was untidy with an empty whisky glass sticky enough to have been used the night before standing near the unopened morning papers. Hearing footsteps on the parquet floor of the hall, Webber was back in the waiting room and reading an old copy of *Collector's Guide* as Maguire entered and greeted him.

He was indeed about sixty and more sombrely and tidily

dressed than Webber had pictured him. He was short and plump rather than fat with bright dark eyes and the quick precise movements of a small wild animal. His hands were neat and delicate. Webber was surprised to see that his fingernails were dirty. In the surgery he placed a carrier bag sprouting a cos lettuce and onions with elaborate care on the floor near his desk and waved Webber to a seat facing him.

"My housekeeper says you've been waiting for some time. Sorry about that, been to a funeral, not one of my failures, poor chap fell downstairs." He changed a short laugh which seemed to take him by surprise into a more becoming cough, sending a sharp burst of Mrs. Thomas's whisky across the desk.

"Now then Inspector, tell me what I can do for you."

The oak chest, until so recently the sad supporter of Rupert's coffin, had been pushed against the wall of the shop where, covered by a clean white sheet from the spare bed, it now bore a happier burden of drinks, and plates of Mrs. Thomas's salty cheese straws to encourage conviviality.

The rain clouds which had provided such a suitably gloomy backcloth for the graveside had now quite disappeared, dispersed by a soft wind from the south, leaving the Suffolk sky bright blue and clear in defiance of the weather forecast. With the shop blinds still reverently drawn the sun had to fight its way in through the fanlight over the door and the holes in the blinds themselves. It cut bright swords of light through the dust and tobacco smoke making the bulbs in the various lampshades look sad and grubby like the exit signs in a country cinema. The shop made a generous annex to the sitting room so that the guests might circulate freely without feeling cramped.

"And you never know," Mrs. Thomas had told Doreen, "someone might fancy something."

Quite a few of the guests did in fact fancy something, and beneath Doreen's shy and becoming acceptance of their condolences and with her senses alerted by two large vodka and tonics, she was considerably surprised by the number of mourners who either hinted delicately at, or openly enquired about, the piece of pottery she had so recently and pleasantly acquired.

Flighty, lazy, and mean, was an incomplete assessment of Doreen's character, for Mrs. Thomas herself was inclined to make snap judgments based on scant evidence and the current condition of her legs. She had not allowed for the effect of Rupert's influence and one thing which Doreen had learned over the years of her marriage was when to keep her mouth shut. She now defended her wicket with all the stubbornness of a dedicated but cautious lady cricketer.

"I think what I shall always remember most about him," Adam Goodman was telling her, "was his kindness. After all we were very much new boys when we first came to Flaxfield and not everyone would have welcomed opposition, but whenever I asked his advice he was always very helpful."

Betsey stood and listened with apprehensively large eyes. He wasn't quite sure of the drift Adam was taking and he very much hoped he wasn't going to overdo it. The only advice Doreen could remember Rupert expressing concerning the future of Adam and his partner had been given to her in private and she didn't think it was intended to be passed on to them. She quite liked the fat floppy one who made her laugh in the butcher's but Adam made her feel uneasy. He was talking about Joseph O'Shea and risking quite a lot for high stakes.

"Nothing marvellous but he got it specially for me and

stupidly I forgot to tell James here who turned it down. I just wondered if by any chance he sold it to you? It's not the profit of course, that's not important, although I'd be happy to see you didn't lose by it, but I like to keep promises, especially to collectors.''

Doreen received and blocked the ball in complete silence which so unnerved Betsey that before Adam could retrieve it and bowl again she had been rescued by a recipe for Betsey's chocolate sponge.

Adam had not been the first of her husband's mourners to approach her. There had been that curious little man in black leather who had plainly not believed her when she had told him she couldn't remember anything like it in the shop. He was now wandering around morosely making notes of all Rupert's price tickets in a grubby little notebook.

The Vicar hadn't even waited for her to deny or confirm its existence.

''Wonderful ham, Welsh-cured your mother tells me. A very distinctive flavour, we don't seem to find it like this locally these days. Now Mrs. Corder,'' he guided her discreetly to the shelter of a long-case clock with his free hand on her elbow.

''Hardly the time or the occasion one would have chosen but you must accept it as well meant advice. Sometimes when one's judgment is clouded by sorrow—''

His advice was to exchange the Pew Group—although he avoided calling it that—for his entire collection. The more stock she could command until such time as she could feel equal to facing the harsh world of the market place the easier would the burden be to bear. She was not to comment now, merely to know that she was not alone, that she had friends who would be happy to place her interests first. It was no more than his simple duty.

She had given him the same shy sad smile that she now gave to Adam.

"Let me get you another drink, and you too, Mr. Trottwood. Isn't it funny, I would never have thought about fresh raspberries instead of cream in a chocolate sponge. Mother dear, Major Goodman and Mr. Trottwood have empty plates."

"It's purely routine," Inspector Webber was telling Dr. Maguire. "I shall have to report to the police medical board at the end of my leave but while I'm away I'm supposed to let them know the name of my local doctor."

Maguire looked down again at the papers Webber had given him. He sat upright holding them daintily like a squirrel with a nut.

"You've read all this, of course?"

"Yes."

"Frighten you?"

"They're not usually so generous with extended sick leave." The funeral party had removed some of Maguire's professional reticence and the routine nature of Webber's visit had given him a distinct feeling of relief. There could have been so many unpleasant reasons why a police inspector should wish to interview an incurious coroner.

"It's mostly balls you know, dressed up a bit. Long words like cholesterol, triglycerides—never heard of them when I qualified. Overweight, well most men are at fifty, I call that normal. Blood pressure's up a bit, so's mine I daresay if I took it." He handed Webber's papers back to him. "Are you staying in Flaxfield then?"

"For a while I thought. I'm at the Bull, I might try and find something to rent later." There was a curious wildness about Maguire's shock of uncombed grey hair, thought

Webber, that reflected his personality more accurately than the funeral suit.

Maguire for his part had noted the unusually pale blue eyes observing him and again found himself grateful that the visit was purely medical.

"Given you a strict diet have they?"

"Pretty strict."

Maguire nodded. "Yes they do that." He produced a bottle of whisky and another glass from the desk. "Welcome to Flaxfield, my first prescription. They're a mixed bunch here, a lot of retired people cursing fixed pensions, refugees from the new Jerusalem." He added some water to the glasses at the small hand basin in the corner. "The locals are a bit close, a crafty lot on the whole. Silly Suffolk they call themselves but they're sharper than they'd like you to think. Cheers; what made you choose Flaxfield for your sabbatical?"

"I was born here," said Webber. "Cheers."

So far the funeral party had been a distinct success even though a few of the guests had left unreasonably early; Miss Hislop succumbing to a headache, Dr. Maguire summoned by a telephone call from his housekeeper and Adam Goodman in a mood of suppressed fury. Among the remaining guests a blissfully happy Mrs. Thomas, fortified by Guinness and elastic, floated like a parody of her dancing youth with her tray of ham sandwiches at the ready and a seraphic smile for all. Doreen alone she avoided. It seemed best. The girl was in one of her moods and determined not to enjoy herself. She was probably jealous. At least Flaxfield was seeing what a funeral should be, and she was a social success whether Doreen liked it or not. Even the vicar had congratulated her before retreating to a secluded corner of the sitting room where he felt happier keeping a protective eye on his wife's consumption of brandy and milk, a beverage suggested by Betsey Trottwood as being both nourishing and respectable. She had already hummed one or two bars of that rather catchy hymn tune and if Christmas was anything to go by he was afraid she might be tempted to dance a little.

Betsey, seeking out Doreen to apologize for his partner's outburst, found her sitting on a Victorian Tudor oak stool forcing her left shoe back on to a foot which didn't welcome it. She hoped he wasn't going to say anything nice about Rupert. He seated himself near her viewing her predicament pleasantly and judicially with his head on one side, an attitude which an American sergeant had once told him looked boyish as indeed it had then.

"I get it sometimes too, only with me it's my right foot. It's too much standing. What you need is a bowl of cold water with ice, or better still, slippers, but you can't very well in here, can you? I see that." His gaze left her foot and assessed the rest of her critically with a look she would have resented from a woman.

"I like the jet beads but I wouldn't have the cameo brooch on the lapel."

"Where should it be?"

"Nowhere. It's too much, dear; one or the other."

The girl needed taking in hand, he'd thought so ever since he'd seen her in the Bull wearing jeans and an angora sweater with bobbles. He leaned forward and for a wild moment in her depressed and nervous state Doreen thought he was going to kiss her.

"Let's go out into the garden," he whispered. "I shall get the giggles if I stay in here much longer; do you good too, you can slip your shoes off."

In the fresh sunlight at the bottom of the strip of garden

stood a wobbly wooden table and garden seat with wrought iron arms like rusty Swiss rolls.

"Now come along, sit comfy and take off the shoes. Never mind the bird shit, it'll brush off and anyway that dress will have to go." He held out the palm of his hand towards her forestalling an objection she found herself too tired and too interested to make. She watched him place a paper plate with sandwiches on the table and produce an almost full bottle of champagne and two glasses from the bulging pockets of his jacket.

"There now, that's better, isn't this fun! Only we mustn't dawdle. Someone's bound to come boring us, they always do."

"I've been drinking vodka," said Doreen eyeing the bubbles dubiously. "Do you think they mix?"

"Yes, of course, silly girl, anything mixes except perhaps green chartreuse and rum. I made myself very poorly with that once, mind you I was upset at the time but I haven't tried it since. Are you sure you won't have a sandwich?" She shook her head. Alone among the mourners she hadn't touched the ham. She knew that it would upset her mother and she had meant it to do so.

Betsey selected a sandwich and settled back comfortably.

"Did you ever see Mrs. Miniver?"

"You mean the film?"

"Umm, I don't know why I suddenly thought of it now. It's the sun I expect. It was always lovely and sunny in Greer Garson's films and she was so brave, she made me cry."

The thought made him wonder what his tears at the graveside had done to the make-up under his eye and gave him time to compose what he wanted to tell her. Somehow it didn't seem a bit odd for Doreen to lend him the mirror from her handbag.

"Oh dear! I thought so. Let's see what you've got." He peered doubtfully at the tube of coloured cream she produced for him and sighed. "Wrong shade for me—and for you," he told her, repairing as much of the damage as he could. He decided that he could best advise her about her make-up in more helpful detail later. There might not be time enough now. "I'm not asking," he said smoothing some of the cream gently under his eye with his little finger, "but I'll tell you this. If I had bought that piece of pottery instead of turning it down, I wouldn't sell it to anyone, not until I'd found out about it—all about it—and how much it was worth. Oh dear! that's worse than ever isn't it?" He moistened another finger in his wine and picked up a dab of dried white bird powder from the table to tone down the orange glow which clashed uncomfortably with the colour of his wig. "There, that's much better, God bless."

She didn't answer and he took a piece of ham from his sandwich thoughtfully licking off the mustard before offering it to Bunter who had come to sit hopefully on the grass in front of them. The cat sniffed at it carefully and thoroughly before making deliberate scratching movements all round it as if to cover and hide it for ever before walking away without once looking back.

"Silly pussy," said Betsey, "you don't know what's good for you."

In the silence the sun warmed their faces and she felt the cool dampness of the grass through her hot stockings. She wondered how he would re-act if she said, "My husband didn't fall by accident. I tripped him deliberately. Tell me about your eye, what made him hit you?" But she kept silent, watching him.

With his eyes closed he stirred some memory for her, an image half forgotten, and then quite suddenly it came to her.

An old newsreel on television, showing women collaborators in France when the Germans had gone. Quite an old woman and they had dragged her from a house and beaten her about the face and made her sit in the sunshine while they had cropped her hair. It was the same hair, the same look of resignation, unresisting and helpless in defeat.

In the shop, Eddie Cabert made bolder by the noise and indifference around him, stretched his arm to its utmost length into the window so that with the extreme tips of his fingers he could reach the price ticket on a copper kettle. Since his movement was limited and awkward he also released the worn catch of the window blind. The explosion of sound as it crashed up to the ceiling stunned the mellow mourners into white-faced silence, while Eddie found himself looking directly into the eyes of Gaylord W. Whitman, Jnr. separated only by the plate glass of the window.

CHAPTER 7

THE SEAT NEAR the war memorial was new since Webber's time; his feet hurt and he was glad to sit on it and rest. His walk round the village after leaving Maguire's surgery had tired him. Flaxfield was still very much as he remembered it as a boy. Not far down the road, round the corner near the paper shop was the terraced house where he had been born and brought up. His father had been a gardener on the estate at Henworth Hall and the name of his elder brother was on the war memorial. Flight Sergeant David Webber.

To be a tired, overweight policeman with a failed marriage, an undistinguished career and a medical report disturbing enough for his superiors to put him out to graze for a month or two should, he reflected, have reduced him to a state of extreme depression. Curiously he felt a distinct lightening of the spirit, but whether he could attribute this to the absence of his wife, his release from office routine, or the doctor's whisky he was not certain. Nor did he care very much. Maguire was right; you could be as healthy as a stud bull and still fall downstairs and break your neck. Freedom was more than a word, it was a late gift to be savoured and enjoyed.

On the other side of the road a group of sombrely dressed people talking rather loudly waited for a very young police constable to hold up the traffic at the pedestrian crossing for them. Somewhat ahead of the main group a clergyman was trying to hurry along his woman companion who seemed reluctant to keep up with him. Webber couldn't distinguish the words of her song but the tune was bright and cheerful and she paused in the middle of the road to execute a few simple dance movements. Folk dancers returning from rehearsal, perhaps. There had been a revival in country folklore since he was a boy, a return to the old virtues of self entertainment. He liked that, it was good to see people happy and laughing together; ordinary people for a change, not part of one of his professional puzzles where the pieces never seemed to fit, not neatly and satisfyingly anyway. The truth was he had lost interest in it all. It wasn't personal anymore, not like it used to be when he started. He had never been first class, he knew that. A little better than adequate perhaps, yes, that was fair, and at least he'd enjoyed it until the computers had tied him to a desk and changed everything. It used to be like flyfishing and now it was just trawling, and they knew he thought that because he'd told them. Perhaps the sick leave was merely an excuse to get rid of him. There had been hints—an early retirement, a pension of sorts, well why not? Somewhere here in Flaxfield perhaps, he'd thought about it. It was tempting. He remembered solitary walks in Henworth Woods as a boy, smoking tobacco stolen from his father in a cheap cherrywood pipe. There had been stories of complaisant girls who wore no knickers. They were rumoured to sit provocatively on low branches of trees;

silent lascivious loreleis. He had never found them and he had remained a pipe-smoking virgin until he had joined the police force and a girl in Coulsdon had told him he had the most beautiful eyes in the world. The night he proposed to her in the doorway of a jeweller's shop in Coulsdon High Street he was listened to in respectful silence by two burglars on the other side of the door who had the decency to hear him out without interrupting. The robbery, unlike the marriage, had been highly successful.

Mrs. Thomas faced the mountain of washing up in the kitchen with positive pleasure; the size of her task was the measure of her success. Flaxfield would remember Rupert's funeral as a social landmark, a standard to aim for on future occasions. There had been an unhappy moment when she had thought that she would be left with quite a lot of food on her hands but once the blind was up she'd had the bright idea of opening the shop door so that passersby could be invited to mingle and pay homage with the last of the mourners until only crumbs and Gaylord Whitman remained.

In the shop, Doreen sat facing him across a small table in the alcove where Rupert had kept his accounts and his reference books. Between them lay an open cheque book and an impressive gold pen. When Mrs. Thomas came in from the kitchen drying her hands they were silent. Sensing the tension in the air she did her best with it.

"There's a man at the back door," she said brightly, "wants a bucket of water for a horse, what shall I say?"

"Ask him to wait," said Doreen extending a hand with a gentle smile. "You must forgive me Mr. . . ." she glanced at his card, "Mr. Whitman, I'll remember all you've said and I'm sure it will make more sense later, but just at present . . ." She let the words fade but kept the smile. Apart from shaking her or hitting her, both of which he found himself longing to do, he could only accept what he prayed was a temporary setback and leave.

Mrs. Thomas did her best to overhear her daughter's conversation with Joseph but it wasn't easy because Doreen had closed the kitchen door, a typical piece of selfish behaviour which had made her mother even more curious about this latest visitor. Definitely not a mourner, not with a tattooed chest and a horse. The keyhole was full of fluff and to blow through it might have attracted attention so she contented herself with pressing her best ear flat against the door and occasionally limping lightly across to the sink to establish a reassuring clink of crockery. What little she managed to hear—odd words and disjointed phrases—made no sense but this minor frustration did little to dampen her happiness, and when the beautiful young man left she was astute enough not to mention that he had forgotten the bucket of water. Nothing could spoil her day, she had not enjoyed herself so much for years. As a widow in Cardiff she had sunk into a routine of mediocrity, her talents unchallenged and unstretched, and she wondered how long she could succeed in extending her visit. Welcomed or not, with Rupert gone Doreen would need a mother's unobtrusive help and guidance. She plunged into the washing up with renewed enthusiasm. She would make herself indispensable, that was the answer, and above all she would remember that Doreen was no longer a teenaged handful but a widow in her own right to be treated with respect and tact.

"Lovely looking boy that, sexy too. Who is he, the milkman?"

"Mr. O'Shea is a runner, Mam. You wouldn't understand. Rupert and I have done business with him for years. He's very useful."

All the same, thought Mrs. Thomas, she's cheered up quite a bit.

Joseph was cheerful, too, that June evening, ambling slowly through the Suffolk lanes with Katie, the sun warm on their backs. Quite apart from her enthusiasm and unexpected sexual talents he genuinely liked Doreen. Young girls were hard work, veering alarmingly from panic to poetry. She was refreshingly direct. Would she see him again? She would certainly, just as soon as she could get rid of her mother. As tidy as that, and would he mind telling her if he'd stolen the little piece of pottery or was it clean? She had no strong feelings either way but now that she was a widow on her own it would be nice to know. Joseph was a sensitive boy and appreciated the same quality in others. He liked the way she had not mentioned her husband's death at their first meeting. It showed delicacy. The article in question, he assured her, he had purchased himself from a thin woman at a garden fête in aid of St. Paul's church. You could almost say it was sanctified. The three little people sitting on the bench, he further assured her, were therefore as clean as a Sunday shirt. He didn't wear Sunday shirts any longer. In England they didn't care what you were or did as long as you weren't black. With a Protestant father and a Catholic mother in Belfast he was intelligent enough to hate everything they both stood for and clear out.

That was six years ago. His sister had taken sides and gone to work in Dublin. Joseph had sailed for England in a cattle boat carrying horses for slaughter in Liverpool. After a crossing with a sea like a Hollywood hurricane he staggered down the gangplank to see the horses stumbling and seasick being herded into the gaping backsides of huge lorries. Without stopping to think he joined the crowd of bellowing and threshing stevedores. The short length of rope he seized to lend authority to his assumed role he casually haltered over the head of one of the horses and led her out of the arc lamps into the dark and pouring rain of the back streets of the Liverpool docks. He was eighteen then. He didn't know how old Katie was.

When they reached the entrance to the overgrown drive that led down to Henworth Hall, the horse turned off the road without being asked and began the last lap of her journey home.

In the evening after telephoning his wife, Webber replaced the receiver with relief and ordered a pint of Adnam's bitter in the bar. In fairness he thought she was probably as relieved as he was himself. Although she had professed mild concern over his medical report she had not objected when he had suggested that some time spent apart might help them both. She had written to her sister the same day inviting her to stay before he could change his mind which he had no intention of doing. Her sister was very like her, even bossier in some ways. They would be perfectly happy comparing symptoms and exchanging sleeping pills like sweets.

The bar of the Bull hadn't filled up for the evening so that he could pick up casual conversations without effort. It reminded him of the early days when he had first worked as a plain clothes man. The fairhaired boy helping the landlord behind the bar Webber recognized as the young policeman he'd seen that afternoon. Well, it was one way of earning a bit more, the wonder was that anyone joined the force at all on that pittance. He looked even younger out of uniform. Probably pure Danish stock, there were more of them in East Anglia than people outside realized. He knew the type well, stubborn and withdrawn unless you caught them on the right foot or behind a bar where you could buy them a drink. He hadn't enjoyed himself so much for years, his Suffolk accent crept back and took colour from the flow around him. The others in the bar relaxed, smelling a dog from their own pack and the gossip of the village unfolded like the pop-up pictures in a child's story book. Thefts of lead from the church roof and copper piping from a barn at Holts Farm; naked witches gambolling with detailed abandon in the services of Satan; the sudden death and alien obsequies of Rupert Corder. He thought of the piles of computerized reports on his desk in Ipswich and watched Constable Burnstead draw up a pint with care and accuracy; more local boy than policeman. Webber sank the level of the brimming mug and paid for it.

"Bit quiet tonight?" he asked.

"That is really quiet tonight," Burnstead agreed, "can't think where they've all got to."

The curse of the Cardiff ham fell upon the funeral guests with impartiality. Nearly all of them managed to get to the lavatory in time although some, disastrously, delayed long enough to try and telephone Dr. Maguire who was himself in no condition to answer. All over Flaxfield, as far out as Lower Henworth, and beyond to the marbled luxury of the Connaught Hotel in London, people in brief moments of peace between peristaltic purges and with the solemnity of the funeral service fresh in their minds made promises they would never keep. Of all the protagonists in the day's drama only Rupert Corder passed the night undisturbed.

Doreen, it is true, would have had a restful night but she had relented enough to sit up and look after her mother. If Mrs. Thomas was really going to die as she kept assuring her daughter through the lavatory door, her funeral, Doreen promised herself, would be spartan. She was now refusing brandy and Bovril alike while Doreen remained within call at Rupert's desk reflecting on the day.

One thing was clear; the piece of pottery was causing a great deal of interest. It must also be—she could not doubt it—very valuable. It was time to do some homework and this, with Rupert's reference books spread out before her and her mother moaning gently in the background she now proceeded to do.

Closeted in the Connaught, Gaylord Whitman wondered miserably where he had gone wrong apart from mistaking a funeral for a wedding party and unexpectedly contracting dysentery. For most of his life his cheque book had been a key which had opened every door. With its aid it had been simple to have Eddie followed. A Pew Group was too important to leave in his hands, the guy wasn't big enough to handle it. It didn't make sense. All antique dealers were sharp and none that he could recall had ever refused to name a price. And yet not once had she even glanced down at the open cheque book, refusing to be drawn. He had accepted food from the woman she claimed was her mother in order to prolong the interview as long as possible—and he'd got nowhere at all. Judging by the rest of the stock she was not a specialist and not every knowledgeable collector had the luck to tempt an inexpert dealer on the day of her husband's funeral. It made her silence inexplicable, worrying and very very frustrating. The great danger in delay was that she would discover how much it was worth.

That was precisely what Doreen had done.

Rupert's books cross referenced to his old sale-room catalogues left no room for doubt. The Pew Group was quite certainly the most valuable object the shop had ever owned.

The curious little group of white salt-glazed figures was as clear in her mind as the photographs on the pages of the books in front of her.

She didn't even need to compare them but it was a luxury she felt she had earned. She crossed to the corner of the shop and opened the door of the cupboard where she had so sensibly hidden it away for safety.

The cupboard was quite empty.

CHAPTER 8

THE RIDGE OF high pressure which had been hovering uncertainly over the Atlantic now took courage and decided to abandon its planned visit to the South of France spreading instead gently across the British Isles and finally coming to rest almost immediately above Flaxfield and Lower Henworth.

"Sixty two cloudy in Nice," announced Mrs. Thomas happily, "and raining in Malaga, there's lovely."

On the fourth day after the funeral she was taking nourishment again and felt recovered enough to spare a thought for her neighbours in Cardiff who had booked their package holidays abroad.

Across the breakfast table Doreen ignored her mother's homemade marmalade and gloomily considered her position. It wasn't in the shop, that was certain. Over-casual enquiries had established that her mother hadn't moved it, therefore someone must have stolen it. The suspects paraded before her and confused her as much as the paperback crime novels that she and Rupert used to take on holiday with them. She had never been able to solve those either. In a paperback it would almost certainly have been the Vicar.

The problem was too big for her and she knew it. It was a job for the police, but suppose they discovered that in spite of his assurances Joseph had stolen it in the first place? Prison for him and returned to its rightful owner that's what, and she wouldn't see a penny of it. She might even be accused of receiving stolen goods. All she had wanted to do was to refuse all offers until she had some idea of what it was worth and then when the time came sell it quietly without a word to anyone and she had been cheated. The more she pondered the more exasperated and frustrated she became.

Petty thief or not the only good thing about the whole wretched business was still Joseph. He was something she thought she had lost forever and she hadn't nearly finished with him yet. There was no reason why she should confuse business with sex. When her mother had gone she would begin to enjoy her new freedom.

"There's a lady here in Bournemouth," announced her mother, "found not guilty of running a brothel and fined five hundred pounds."

The sun reverted to its rightful position in the morning sky illuminating Mrs. Thomas's newspaper so that she could read it without her glasses. It made her feel young and she hoped Doreen would notice but she didn't.

"You mean guilty, Mam."

"No I don't. 'When asked by the judge why she had named her establishment "The Stimulating Sauna," she replied that it referred to quality of the girls' conversations.' "

"So how could they fine her?"

"They got her for not paying VAT, poor dab. Thank God

your Auntie Blodwen retired before they started all that non-sense.''

Doreen looked across at her mother contentedly browsing through her newspaper with a sudden surge of affection, even of admiration for her. Infuriating and embarrassing as she was, Doreen knew that her mother had always acted in what she felt to be her daughter's interest whether Doreen agreed or not. She had never openly referred to her sister's occupation, although Doreen knew perfectly well how her Auntie Blodwen had earned a modest fortune in Cardiff's Tiger Bay, enough certainly to buy a house in London and retire in comfort. When Doreen was a schoolgirl and her closest and most hated friends had informed her of their parents' gossip about her aunt, she had retaliated by rattling every real and invented skeleton in their own cupboards, but she had never been able to ask her mother if what they said was true. She knew that her mother and aunt had always been close even though their lives had divided, and she had preferred to leave the question unasked, thinking that one day they would tell her themselves. As an adolescent her fantasy had invented the scene many times. Her mother pleading with her to abandon her rough boyfriends with the exciting motor bikes and Auntie Blodwen in tears confessing that in just such a way she had begun her luxurious life of shame in Cardiff docks. With the passing years and her marriage to Rupert the likelihood of such revelations had become remote until now suddenly and delicately, and as casually as a reference to the weather over a pot of runny home-made marmalade, her mother had said it quite openly.

In fact it was a mistake. Mrs. Thomas had never meant to say a word and she could scarcely believe that she had done so. She hoped that if she held the newspaper firmly enough Doreen would not pursue it, being too preoccupied with her own worries and in particular that silly little piece of white china which seemed to have upset her so much. In this she was mistaken: there are priorities. In spite of herself she sneaked a quick look at Doreen over the top of the paper and seeing her daughter's face on the edge of open laughter she was the first to break.

"Oh God! She'd kill me if she knew." When Doreen laughed, thought her mother, she looked quite different, it was like seeing her sister Blodwen again when they were younger.

"You musn't laugh, you know it's not for talking about," she said wiping her eyes on a corner of the table cloth.

"Auntie Blod wouldn't mind, she's tougher than you and that's saying something. Anyway, I've known for years. Why wasn't it for talking about?"

"You were only a child, how could I?"

"When I was older you could have."

"Oh come on, fair play, you know what Dada was like. Chapel and pigeons, and I had to fit in. He was afraid for you. God knows you were wild enough as it was; he was frightened it was in the blood. He made us promise we'd never say a word, it was the only way he'd let us see each other."

"I always remember her clothes," said Doreen taking a spoonful of marmalade as a gesture and proof of genuine interest. "What was it like in Cardiff?"

"Clean as a pin, bright but not tarty. Tasteful. She always reckoned she gave a service. It says Social Worker in her passport."

When Mam laughed, thought Doreen, she looked exactly like her sister, heaving and happy.

"I'm surprised Dada used to let her come and see us at all."

72

"Everyone has a price," said her mother, "and Dada's was pigeons—some lovely birds she gave him. Yes, poor love, she used to like coming for a rest. Her legs weren't as bad as mine but it's in the family."

Doreen watched her as she folded the sticky newspaper and lifted the lid of the teapot to see if it would stand any more water. The familiarity of the action took her back to her childhood and the times she had sat watching her mother lifting the lids of a thousand teapots through the years. She had sat as she sat now across the table wanting to talk and confide in her, and yet always stopping and drawing back.

If Doreen thought that her mother was unaware of the moat between them she was mistaken, but Mrs. Thomas was afraid of further estrangement. The girl was edgy, a wrong move now and she might even be asked to leave and go home to Cardiff. She wouldn't go, of course, but it was better not to be asked. There were several moves open to her and she rejected them. Direct questions, however tempting, could wait until she had consolidated her position and felt more secure, and things looked decidedly more cheerful. Some of the tension and gloom had lifted, the weather and her stomach were more settled, and Doreen had laughed. If she wasn't rushed and frightened she might lower the draw-bridge.

"Good God, half past ten! This won't pay the old woman her ninepence, me chatting away, stopping your working. Now I don't want you getting overtired, just tell me what you want and I'll do the shopping."

She considered giving Doreen a motherly kiss as she went to collect the shopping bag but decided against it and contented herself with an affectionate hand on her shoulder as she passed behind her chair. The gesture proved unexpectedly useful since one of her legs had gone to sleep and Doreen became a temporary crutch as she limped to the door. Doreen's self pity welled up, disguising itself as concern for her mother's lameness and without pausing to think she led her gently back to the table and across the moat.

It was more than her mother had dared hope for after the fiasco of the ham. She sat down quietly, refreshed the teapot and listened.

In the days that followed, the sun shone from a postcard-blue sky with no sign of clouds. Mrs. Thomas had been among the very first to recover from the effects of her sandwiches (many people thought unfairly and said so). Gradually, however, the warmth of the sun brought pale faces to windows and then tempted them into the open to move around Flaxfield with a greater sense of comfort and safety. Far from avoiding them Mrs. Thomas deliberately sought them out to apologise, comparing case histories and symptoms in detail and listening more sympathetically than Dr. Maguire had time or inclination for. She became a woman with a mission, but behind the gentle concern her spirits sank. Not by deed or word or hint of mind was she able to add one scrap of knowledge to the one certain fact that one of the funeral guests was a thief and had stolen a rare and valuable piece of china from her daughter's shop. Cardiff loomed uncomfortably close.

"It's no use, Mam, we'll have to leave it. I shall just have to manage. I've still got the shop haven't I?"

"You don't even know how much he's left you apart from that. What did the solicitor say?"

"It's all got to be sorted out, he's going to write to me. I honestly don't know, Rupert was very close. You mustn't worry, I'm very lucky really, I'll write and let you know everything I promise."

Time was running out.

The vicar, having taken his wife some lemon tea and dry toast in bed, now selected the most comfortable hassock in the north chantry chapel.

"I expect you've already got a pretty good general idea of how things stand, Lord, but I thought perhaps you might like a few details. By the way, you'll be pleased that Joan and I seem to have got over the worst of the diarrhoea although it has taken longer with her, what she really needs is a holiday of course. However, that's just not possible I'm afraid. Now, about the Ministry of the Environment and the money they are supposed to give for the repair of outstanding churches. Lord, it said in the *Daily Telegraph* that they had seven hundred and fifty thousand pounds to give away this year and that one should apply for a form from one's Archdeacon. Now I spoke to Archdeacon Gray on the telephone the other day and I got a very strong impression that he wasn't going to be very encouraging, although he did promise to send me a form. He seems to think that St. Peter's might not be considered outstanding enough. I don't know if you can remember him at all, he came to us quite recently from Lincoln where I believe he was known as the Lincolnshire Handicap. Lord I pray, and commit the form to your care and judgment." For a moment he wondered if he should mention the Corders' shop and the tantalizing mystery of the Pew Group but gallantly decided not to press his luck and besides, he had promised Joan he would do the weekend shopping.

High on the roof of St. Peter's an old workman employed by Mr. Wilson the church architect to confirm his original measurements paused to light his pipe and survey the warm peace of the village below. It was a survey which gave him more pleasure than the one he was being paid for. In all the years he had been checking Mr. Wilson's figures he had only occasionally found him to be even slightly inaccurate. For a long time now he had found it easier simply to copy his employer's figures on to his work sheet. The new fangled metric system was quite confusing enough without further complicating the issue by pretending to understand it and it gave him more time to pursue his hobby of bird watching. He could have told Joan Coley that the birds which flew over the vicarage were rooks not ravens but the information would have meant little to her. Some birds simply left larger messes on her windows than others and some had to be rescued from Bunter if she could corner him in time, but she never knew their names.

She was at that moment lying gratefully on her bed thankful for the lemon tea and dry toast which William had brought her and happily unaware that three out of the four clues she had solved for him in the *Telegraph* crossword were quite wrong. She was also so glad to be alone and left to recover undisturbed that it occurred to her to doubt the usefulness of her own role over the years as sick visitor to the parish.

The old workman watched approvingly as a church sparrow repaired its nest beautifully without the least knowledge of centimetres or inches. He watched it fly down to the churchyard below in search of new building material. Outside in the road the vicar and a dumpy little woman with bright pink legs were deep in conversation.

''She's a changed woman, very disturbed; I'm her mother, I can tell.''

''It's been a great strain for her,'' said William.

"Something's gone, she's lost something."

"It sounds glib I know but time does heal. The memory of Mr. Corder is so fresh—"

"I don't mean that. She's lost something from the shop—stolen." It was too late for finesse. If Doreen wouldn't act it was up to her, she had nothing to lose.

"Oh dear, how very distressing. Did she by any chance say what it was?"

"A piece of china of some sort. Three people sitting on a sofa or something like that. It's upset her, I'd better get back to her, poor girl. I think that Irish boy comes into it somewhere too."

"I wonder if you'd care for a quick cup of coffee?" said William. "My wife is really so much better today and she makes rather good coffee. She'll be delighted to see you."

CHAPTER 9

IT SAID A great deal for Joan Coley that she received William's news that Mrs. Thomas had dropped in for coffee without flinching.

"I'm in the kitchen," she heard her visitor call out as she came downstairs with William. She felt decidedly shaky but determined to forgive, and to avoid any reference to the cause of her recent agonies.

"My God, you look peeky girl, there's a shame! I'll kill that bloody pork butcher—forgive language but we've all got troubles, now sit there tidy, shan't be a tick."

"Mrs. Thomas please! You really shouldn't be doing the washing up. I'd no idea there was so much. William, however could you have used so many things?"

"Don't be silly, girl. It's nearly done, I'd have been over sooner but I've been glued to the lav myself. Kettle's on, where's your coffee?"

"I'm terribly sorry but I'm afraid—I mean William should have known."

"Forgot to buy it? I know, men are hopeless with shopping, never mind, plenty here." She dived into her carrier bag like a terrier, producing coffee, fresh bread, butter and various tins. "When did you eat last?"

"No honestly, it's terribly kind of you but I've had breakfast. William will tell you."

Under her gimlet eye William faltered. "She did manage some dry toast and lemon tea this morning."

"Good God Almighty, you'll be lying out there next to Doreen's Rupert on dry toast. Now don't move while I just dry up and then food. Lovely, I'm quite peckish myself. Mr. Coley tell you Doreen's gone off up the mountain?"

"Up the mountain?"

"That's what I used to have to tell her Dada. I know the signs."

William was more concerned with her other news. "My dear, something rather disturbing has happened. Mrs. Corder appears to have had something stolen from the shop. Good gracious, my dear Mrs. Thomas! I couldn't possibly manage all that and I'm sure Joan—"

Joan, however, was responding to treatment. She found it difficult to feel like an invalid with this woman bouncing about her kitchen as though she'd been in it for years. There was something infectious about her, she thought, and then had to stop herself laughing aloud at the inappropriate word, reassuring herself that Mrs. Thomas's hands would certainly be clean after all that washing up and the corned beef on her plate she had seen come straight from a tin. She was suddenly very hungry.

"You said that Mrs. Corder seemed upset. I do hope the piece wasn't very expensive?" Expensive was quite clever, he thought—more precise than valuable.

"I shouldn't be surprised," said Mrs. Thomas, settling

herself comfortably at the kitchen table and pouring more H.P. sauce on her corned beef than she had intended. "I shouldn't be surprised if it wasn't worth hundreds." Hundreds sounded more encouraging than thousands.

"But she didn't mention any particular sum?"

"She's a funny girl, can't get close to her, never could. She won't have the police, won't hear of it. Coffee all right for you?"

"Thank you, delicious, but surely she should have informed the police at once?"

"Of course she should, but no. And don't go telling anyone, Mam, she said. It's private. She didn't mean you, of course."

"She's quite sure it hasn't been mislaid?"

"We've had the place upside down. She put it in a cupboard she says, and it's gone. Think back Doreen, I said. Think back girl, could you have slipped it in with Rupert and forgotten?"

William heard quite clearly what she had said but he began to feel the thread of her argument slipping away from him and it was far too important to let that happen.

"Yes quite, I see," he said slowly. "You mean actually in the coffin?"

"That's right, you know, like you do, a little something for company."

William didn't know. He knew that such things were practised extensively in ancient Egypt but had not realized that the custom had filtered down to the Welsh valleys. It raised problems. His mind raced ahead, worrying at them like stubborn clues in a crossword, a world in which there was no place for ethics. Official exhumation was out of the question. He was almost certain that permission for that would involve more red tape than even Archdeacon Gray had prophesied for the government grant. It would have to be arranged privately. A long, dark night's work, messy but necessary, and if by some sad chance detected he would claim that he had surprised some hideous ceremony in the act, those notorious Suffolk witches perhaps, and that he was reverently restoring the sacrilege.

"How jolly interesting," said Joan feeling enormously improved.

"Goodness, I did enjoy that. Do tell me Mrs. Thomas, unless you'd rather not of course, but when Mr. Thomas died . . . ?"

"In with him you mean? Pipe and tobacco, of course, asked for them himself. I used to say he might not need matches but I put them in just the same. I sold all his pigeons—he had some lovely birds and I needed every penny."

"Exactly," said William abandoning the gaping grave with relief. "So that Mrs. Corder, however distraught, would hardly have buried such a valuable piece of pottery. It wouldn't make sense."

"That's another thing," said Mrs. Thomas, wiping the last of the sauce from her plate with a piece of bread reserved for that purpose, "she won't tell me how much he left, apart from the shop, pretends it all has to be sorted out with the books and the solicitor." The import of this speech should have left her face sulky and suspicious but she beamed happily at Joan and William over remains of the meal.

"I'm not that daft, she knows but she won't tell, crafty madam," she nodded towards the dirty plates. "Manage these? Yes, I'm sure you can."

"Yes, of course, I feel so much better. William you must try and help, there must be something you can do."

"I suppose you could call it fringe medicine but I prefer to call it common sense." Dr. Maguire divided the remaining claret between Webber's glass and his own, watching with pleasure as the warm afternoon sun made the colour of the wine dance across the white cloth which covered the grime of the garden table. His glass was so full that Webber spilt a little on the cloth as he lifted it.

"Don't worry, it will only give Mrs. Clifton pleasure, I promise you. She warned me the table was too wobbly to have lunch on. I've already made sure of a few coffee stains so that will make her day. She's easily satisfied."

Webber knew that Maguire enjoyed his company, seeking him out at the Bull in the evenings and sometimes, like today, insisting that he came to the house for a meal. He wasn't sure whether he liked the man as a person or whether he simply enjoyed the doctor's general air of irreverence for his profession.

"There must be a good case for preventative medicine though?"

"About as successful as crime prevention I'd say—a limited success rate. I reckon about 80 per cent of cases cure themselves unless you start probing and pulling them about. That's only common sense again, the rest of it's nearly all up here." He tapped his mop of hair. "They say I'm a good doctor, you know."

"And are you?"

Maguire laughed delightedly. "Yes, John, bloody good. I listen to them for one thing, chaps in London haven't got enough time for that any more. I'm really doing what Coley's lot used to do, it's the confessional again with pink pills instead of penance."

"Or red wine?"

"One of my best drugs."

"To be taken with the rest of your prescription to complete the cure."

"You mean my advice about retiring? Oh Lord yes—but you know that anyway or you wouldn't have come down here. You only needed someone to confirm it."

You had to hand it to him, Webber thought, he lived up to his image of universal counsellor. His own training had been geared to produce a quite different image. You sought facts; opinions and judgments you left to others.

His first thought when Maguire had told him he ought to retire was to believe his advice was purely medical, a gentle hint that since his time was short he should enjoy it while he could. The doctor had made it plain that he believed the reverse to be true. He said it again now.

"Keep on with that desk life and you'll never see your pension anyway, so you might as well take what they'll give you and clear out."

"Another refugee cursing a fixed pension?"

"Refugees may be poor but they escape the gas ovens. Damn it, John, you haven't even got a marriage to hold you back except in name anyway; make both the police and your wife quite happy to part amicably with you, one will give you a pension and the other has enough money of her own. Never saw such a neat equation in my life. Yes, Mrs. Clifton, what is it?"

"Mrs. Thomas wants to see you, doctor."

"Surgery five o'clock, she knows that."

"She says it's private and won't take a minute."

"I'll go," said Webber.

"No stay, she might well be a mass murderer. You see how useful you could be to us all."

Mrs. Thomas bounced across the lawn with determination. If the church couldn't help then the medical profession might. Like the vicar, Dr. Maguire knew everyone in Flaxfield; he'd certainly known everyone at the funeral party. It was a long shot but he might have some ideas, anyway it was better than sitting back and doing nothing like Doreen. Doreen, she knew, would be furious with her but the more she became involved the less likely she was to find herself marooned and lonely in Cardiff. The pleasure of greeting pasty-faced neighbours from chilly Spain would be small compensation for the social possibilities of Flaxfield. Besides with Rupert gone Doreen needed her; she might not think so but she did. Brushing aside Webber's renewed offer to leave, Mrs. Thomas gave the facts neatly and concisely. Webber was rather impressed with her; she would have made a good witness, he thought, a bit garrulous but nothing that a good counsel couldn't cope with.

"I'm flattered of course," said Maguire, "but it really isn't my line of country at all. It is true, as you say, that I know everybody but you could hardly expect me to say 'I'll bet it was old so-and-so I've been treating him for kleptomania for years.' "

Mrs. Thomas looked at the twinkling dark eyes coldly. She'd made a mistake, and presented herself as a fool into the bargain. Somehow at the party he'd seemed different, as though he would be kind and helpful. That was her own fault, she'd been too generous with the refreshments, not that, now she came to think of it, he had waited for her to refill his glass. He'd left early too, supposing—black doubt descended upon her, after all what made doctors, or even vicars for that matter, so special that they could be trusted with confidences?

Mrs. Thomas went quite pale and, rising to her feet, gave

her dress a good pull-down in front to restore her composure.

"Yes of course, there's silly I am. Well, sorry to disturb. I'll get off then."

Until he spoke she hadn't looked at Webber properly, she had been carried impetuously along with her story like a little girl in a fairground desperately rolling pennies down a shute, believing that one of them would surely land in the centre of a square and magically restore her dwindling fortune. The man's eyes she saw now were of an exceptionally pale blue, they weren't twinkling maliciously but looked gentle and kind.

"What I don't quite understand," said Webber, "is why your daughter hasn't reported her loss to the police."

Mrs. Thomas didn't understand that clearly either. Doreen had been unspecific on the point and she had not pressed her. You didn't question Doreen's confidences, God knows they were rare enough; you accepted them gratefully and did what you could to help.

Bending was not a movement that came easily to her but she retrieved her handbag from the lawn by the side of her chair without grunting.

"Funerals and police, it's not nice is it? It might only be a joke." It didn't sound at all convincing but with the gentle pale blue eyes looking straight at her it was the best she could do.

"However," said Maguire who had remained seated when Webber had risen politely with Mrs. Thomas, "it seems that the police now know about it, nice or not. I should have explained, perhaps, that Mr. Webber here is a police officer, a Detective Inspector no less."

Years of practice had taught Webber to conceal anger, it was seldom productive. He smiled amiably and naturally.

"Don't worry Mrs. Thomas, your conversation was quite private you know, not what we call an official complaint at all."

"You mean you won't have to report it?"

"That's quite right and in any case Dr. Maguire wasn't strictly accurate just now." He paused long enough to watch the doctor's face before he continued. "He doesn't know about it yet so he didn't mean to mislead you but he should have said ex-Detective Inspector because I'm now retired. I was about to tell him when you came along. So you see," he said, "you've simply been chatting to neighbours and neighbours ought to help each other, don't you think?"

Chapter 10

Webber was enjoying himself. For the first time in years he felt in command of his own affairs. And it had been so simple. He could have wished, perhaps, that his wife or his erstwhile colleagues had made more than token gestures of regret at his decision to abandon them for ever and go his own way but he had not really expected it and he was too much of a realist not to recognize that their relief was probably as great as his own.

He was lucky in that the practical problems had been almost non-existent. The house in which he had been little more than a lodger for years was rented, as all their homes had been as he had moved from post to post. His wife's father's money, which she had inherited, would be ample for her needs. His pension and what little he had been able to accumulate by saving and the occasional judicious acceptance of safe bribes when opportunity had arisen would allow him to live, if not in luxury, then in reasonable comfort. He might even be able to find a small cottage he could afford. His wife and computers were in the past; he had come home. It wasn't the home he remembered, Maguire had been right about that, but it was where he wanted to be more than anywhere else. His offer to help Mrs. Corder and her mother was a token, a gesture of thanksgiving. Flaxfield might be full of foreigners but it was still a place where people were important and neighbours gave each other what help they could with whatever skills they could command. Miss Hislop arranged the flowers in church, not always, he gathered, to everyone's complete satisfaction, but she did her best. The chances of solving the theft of the Pew Group were not very bright but he was determined to try. He might be lucky. Like Miss Hislop he would do his best.

He stood at the end of the private drive which had brought him from the main Saxmundham road to a point where Henworth Hall lay before him resting in the childhood sunshine of an English June, framed like an old print by the overhanging trees which gave way to the vast overgrown lawns and the house itself. The drive had been longer than he had remembered it and one of his toes had developed a blister, giving his walk over the mossy stones a curiously dainty but determined progress. The Hall had absorbed most of the fashionable styles since it was built in 1540 until, in the late eighteenth century it had become predominantly but modestly Palladian. It stood in sad need of repair, in a landscape arranged inevitably by Capability Brown.

Doreen had not shown any great enthusiasm but had accepted both her mother's explanation and Webber's assurance that the investigation was sensible and necessary. She had been decidedly reticent about the possible value of the missing article, as she called it, but almost without her realizing it Webber had extracted the story of the garden fête. She didn't know where Mr. O'Shea lived but his story had been readily confirmed when Miss Hislop had been identified as the thin woman. Yes, Miss Hislop remembered it very well indeed, the young man was quite right, she had not liked him very much but he was telling the truth and she also remembered that the piece of pottery had been in a mixed box of oddments that had been given to the garden fête committee by Lady Ormundham of Henworth Hall.

The heavy stone portico above the door looked decidedly unsafe and Webber hoped that he wouldn't have to stand underneath it too long before someone came to admit him. The last time he had stood there he had been a child of six holding his mother's hand and excited about the Christmas party. They used to ask all the children on the estate until you were six; after that you were too old. He could just remember the old man, he'd died only a few years ago and Webber had read his obituary in *The Times*. Sir George Ormundham C.V.O., M.C., the last of his generation, a vice-lieutenant of Suffolk and sometime chairman of the county council, he was 87. Tried to save the railway and the post office and the village school but they'd all had to close. He was lucky to go, thought Webber, before Henworth Hall itself collapsed about him. Lady Ormundham was a dimmer memory, she must be very old now.

She wasn't old at all, well perhaps about his own age and just now he felt quite young. She had come to the door herself and he liked her at once. It was an unremarkable face in its separate features but the sheer weight of spontaneous happiness came bubbling up behind everything she said so that she seemed not merely an attractive personality but positively beautiful. The fact that she limped and used a stick to help her walk did nothing to dispel this original impression. She paused in her progress across the hall so that she could wave the stick like an extended arm to emphasize either some object about her or some point in her almost non-stop monologue.

"Is it Inspector or mister? It doesn't matter does it, you phoned first and that's always such a comfort. I do try not to be in to some people, poor dears. Inspector I think is nicer. Well, labels are useful aren't they? I should keep Inspector, I really would. I think we'd better use the little drawing room, it's farther to walk but I don't trust that." She waved the stick up at the domed Italianate skylight above the hall. "I don't trust that glass, this sun is shrinking the putty."

Webber remembered when the Christmas tree heavy with presents had almost reached up as far as the dome. Once he had been given some modelling clay in sticks of different colours. He saw it and smelt it again across the years.

He hadn't planned to conduct the interview with one of his feet bare but she had noticed him limping and had dealt with it as efficiently as if the Christmas party had never finished, producing a neat square of Elastoplast to cover the raw knuckle of his toe.

"I should leave your sock off for a while, let it set for a bit. Now let me think, yes, that sounds right to me, a white pottery thing, people sitting on a sort of bench, quite right, I never cared for it. Why do you ask?"

"It seems it finished up in Mrs. Corder's antique shop and might have been stolen. It's rather upset her."

"Well, I don't wonder, how very unpleasant for her on top of everything else, rather odd too."

"Odd?"

"Yes because—oh dear just look at that awful dog! I am sorry, she's mad for bare feet, always has been. Hannah get off! Pull her tail."

Webber compromized by putting his sock and shoe back before the yellow labrador puppy could lick the plaster off.

"You said something was odd."

"Ah yes, it's nothing really but I remember her husband mentioning it on his last visit. He used to come up occasionally and try and buy things, sometimes he'd take a photograph, one of those quick Polaroid things, you know the ones?" Webber nodded. "I'm sorry he fell but he really wasn't very nice."

"And you wouldn't sell it to him?"

She produced a man's handkerchief from the sleeve of her cashmere sweater and gave her nose a good sensible no-nonsense blow, her eyes laughing at Webber over the top of it as she did so.

"Well really he was the most awful little creep, you know! It was a bit difficult to get rid of him because he'd been quite thick with my husband in the old days. He knew my husband's first wife too, he used to do the insurance valuations in the days when they could afford insurance. But no, I never sold him anything. My husband used to sometimes and I didn't much care for that but he said it didn't matter because they were nearly all fakes. How's the toe?"

"It's fine thank you, a great relief. I don't quite understand when you say fakes."

"Well copies then, paintings, bits of porcelain and so on. I think all the good stuff went years ago. A place like this needs money, Inspector."

Webber nodded thoughtfully letting his gaze rest on the flaking paintwork and the threadbare velvet of the window seat.

"Did he make you a definite offer for it?"

"Yes something daft, five pounds or something like that. I remember thinking I'd rather give it to the garden fête. I believe it did quite well, or the Bring and Buy stall did, anyway."

As she talked, Webber was aware that she was regarding him closely as though trying to remember him from some other time when they'd met and talked, but he knew his memory was one of his strong points and that she must be mistaken.

"Why would anyone steal something like that?" she asked suddenly. "It was rather a horrid little piece I thought. It didn't have a mark or anything, do you think they thought it was Chelsea or something really important?"

"Someone must have wanted it quite badly," said Webber, "to take it from a cupboard in the middle of a crowded funeral party. I don't know yet but I think it might have been more valuable than you thought. If you distrusted Corder, didn't it occur to you to find out more about it?"

She shook her head. "Not really. I might have been suspicious if he'd offered me a lot for it but as it was I never gave it a thought. I suppose Corder bought it from the garden fête?"

"I rather think he was dead by then," said Webber mildly. "No, someone else bought it and then sold it apparently to Mrs. Corder later."

"Oh well, good luck to them," said Lady Ormundham using her stick to get up from her chair. "At least the church organ got something out of it. No, I'm all right thank you. I manage fairly well and you get used to it. There are worse things than arthritis, thank God, and I'm progressing. Last winter I had to use two sticks, it must be the hot sun. Listen, don't rush off unless you must. Let's sit out on the terrace and drink some beer. Have you got a list of everyone at the funeral? I must say it's rather interesting isn't it? Oh Hannah, you are a very boring dog. Give it to me at once!" But the labrador puppy, sensing dispossession, disappeared purposefully through the door.

"I expect it was someone's shoe," said Lady Ormund-ham philosophically. "It's part of her foot complex, I'm afraid. I believe she visits most of the tenants on the estate, she wheedles her way in and then pinches their shoes."

"Do you have many tenants?" asked Webber as they found some chairs in the sun on the broad terrace and he poured the beer he had carried out for her.

"Yes it works quite well really, they don't all have jobs on the estate, of course. I couldn't pay them if they did but the rents are low and quite a few of them lend a hand because of that and some of the wives come up and help in the house, rearranging the dust and so forth. Most of the rooms are closed up now, of course; it's rather sad really. When I first came it was quite something."

"I can remember it a little," he said, and found himself telling her. She could listen as well as talk, drawing him out and chuckling delightedly.

"Christmas parties! Ah that was very grand! No I never made that. I came on the scene much later, I came as a nurse originally, a big step up for me, local girl from the cottage hospital. She was very frail, poor dear and then when she died I stayed on to look after Sir George. I was very fond of them both."

Webber sipped his beer and looked out over the stone balustrade grey-green with lichen and beyond the lawns to where the first circle of trees stood like policemen with linked arms keeping back the crowd of Henworth Woods.

"What do you think will happen to the house?"

"I shall keep it of course—even if it falls down I shall keep it. I think that's why he married me." She laughed. "Well that and the nursing. We had a lot in common. He knew I loved Henworth and wouldn't let it go without a fight. We hoped the National Trust might take it but I don't think they're going to. We nearly got a girls' school to take it on but they panicked when Labour got in. Perhaps it's just as well, think of the changing room on a day like this!''

Webber smiled and thanked her for the beer. He hadn't got very far but at least he knew where the Pew Group had come from. Where it was now was another matter.

''I shan't get up,'' she said, ''I'm too lazy and the sun is such a treat, sooner or later someone will bring me a sandwich or something. You know, the secret is to let people help you, it gives great pleasure. I've seen both sides and I know.''

''I'll remember that.''

''Yes do, and will you come and tell me if you discover anything?—especially if it's only gossip, that's always so much more fun.''

He grinned. ''I promise, and thank you again for the beer.''

She held on to his outstretched hand for a moment looking hard into the pale blue eyes.

''That's right—quite right, we locals must stick together, we're a dying breed, most of the village seems full of foreigners, have you noticed that? Yes of course you have.'' She released his hand. ''Oh dear, you're leaving far too soon and there's a lot I wanted to ask you but I mustn't be selfish and it can wait. Where did you park your car by the way, is it round the back?''

''I didn't bring it. I left it at the Bull, I thought the walk would be pleasant. I'm afraid I'd forgotten how far it is out here. I'll catch the bus into Flaxfield if I hurry—that is of course if there still is a bus?''

''You're lucky—it's every other day and this is it—you should be in good time too.''

''You know,'' said Webber, allowing a little of his official technique to creep into his manner, "you may think you recognize me from the old days, when we were children perhaps, but my memory is very good and I'm sure we never knew each other."

"Oh no, I know that," said Lady Ormundham. "No, no, we never met, but I used to know your brother rather well. We didn't tell anyone but we hoped we were going to marry."

Chapter 11

Mrs. Thomas sat alone in the corner of the bar of the Bull drinking her third glass of Guinness and beginning to cheer up. Doreen had not asked her to go out for the evening but she had suggested very strongly that she might have some important business and Mrs. Thomas had taken the hint. On the whole, relations between mother and daughter had been less strained than Mrs. Thomas had feared since she had forced Doreen's hand by introducing Inspector Webber into the affair and she wasn't going to press her luck by complaining if Doreen wanted to behave like a tart and call it business.

Above her head hanging on rusty hooks were two elaborate corn dollies, their convoluted plaited forms mutely invoking the blessing of forgotten gods for fertility in the fields and for a generous supply of village children to clear them of stones for tuppence a week. On the corner wall across the table a bright-eyed conceited racing pigeon posed smugly in lurid water colours surrounded by an impressive list of past triumphs. Mrs. Thomas regarded it fondly. It reminded her not so much of Mr. Thomas but of the time when he had been confined to bed with 'flu and she had been pleasured, unexpectedly but delightfully amid a flurry of feathers in the pigeon cot at the bottom of the tiny garden by the assistant manager of Stead and Simpsons, a pigeon fancier with wider interests and initiative. The memory completed the restoration of her spirits and sat happily upon the foundation laid by the Guinness. On her way to the ladies' lavatory she ordered another which she collected on her way back and carried elegantly to her corner seat where she was delighted to find Webber sitting with a pint of beer before him and two large suitcases on the floor near his chair.

"Well!" she beamed. "I asked for you earlier but they said you were out. Been shopping?"

"I needed a few more clothes. It's always the same on holiday isn't it? You either bring too much or too little. Luckily I'm not too far away."

She nodded, settling happily into the Windsor chair, her evening retrieved from boredom, and applied herself to her glass. Some women, thought Webber, would not have been content with such a bald statement but would have poked and pried into intimate personal details and he liked her for her restraint. In fact, Mrs. Thomas had no need to ask questions, she had already discovered everything she wanted to know from Dr. Maguire's housekeeper Mrs. Clifton, in whom she had early recognized a rich source of interesting information. She was fully aware of Webber's private circumstances and content to confine her enquiries to the more immediate problem of the missing Pew Group. The heat wave which remained unmoved over the whole of Suffolk made the bar as warm as it had been in the day so that all the windows were wide open to catch any faint breeze in the summer night.

"What do you think?" she asked, "will she get it back?"

Webber set his tankard down carefully. "Or do you mean," he said, "would she be more likely to get it back if she made a full scale fuss and reported it officially?"

"What, to that?" Mrs. Thomas said scornfully nodding towards the bar where Constable Burnstead was bringing all his charm to bear on some village girls who might or might not have been eighteen.

"It wouldn't stay with him, you know," said Webber loyally. "That's only the first link, he's all right for petty theft and driving without lights. You'd get a couple of bright lads down from Ipswich, reports to all the antique dealers in the country—abroad even, sale-rooms, collectors, Interpol, the lot."

"And then they'd find it?"

"Yes they might—or they might just frighten someone so much that they'd sit quiet on it for years."

"And on your own?"

He had intended to have only one drink before taking his cases upstairs and unpacking. Instead he refilled their glasses at the bar.

"When I was a young man," he said, "I really wasn't half bad. You never heard of the Gower case?"

She shook her head.

"It wasn't one of the biggest but it made the Sunday papers. Gower was the branch manager of a bank in a small place not much bigger than Flaxfield. He cleaned it out and disappeared with his mistress, a local barmaid called Poppy. I was the village copper." Webber's blue eyes shone with the memory. "It was really very exciting, Scotland Yard murder squad, reporters everywhere."

"The murder squad?"

"Before they left," said Webber, "they burnt the house down with his wife in it. We found her wedding ring but not much else. It was a good job, very thorough—we only found the ring with a sieve."

"No bones?" asked Mrs. Thomas.

Webber gazed at her approvingly.

Mrs. Thomas waited, conserving her Guinness.

"Not even little tiny bits—it was a really good fire."

"The Yard were very thorough," said Webber. "The girl had an older sister in America, one of the G.I. Brides. They went over and questioned her and they went to South Africa where Gower had some contacts through the bank but they didn't find them—not there anyway."

"But they did find them?"

"Yes, or to be honest," said Webber modestly, "I found them. It wasn't really all that clever. I asked Mrs. Gower where they were when she came back about a year later, looking for her dog. It ran away on the night of the fire," he explained, "but one of the locals looked after it."

"Good God, she must have been mad to come back."

"You couldn't put it in a play," Webber agreed, "people wouldn't believe it. She came back in dark glasses and a new Citroën. She even had a new lead ready for the dog. She loved her dog. She never turned a hair when I called her Mrs. Gower although I admit she was wearing a wig."

"What made you so sure?" asked Mrs. Thomas.

"I always thought she might come back. She was a hard woman, very cool, I knew she could murder, but not Gower, all he wanted was out. She came home early and found him writing a note for her. Another five minutes and he and Poppy would have got away. She shot them and dropped them down a pot hole on the moors—not the money, of course, she kept that; then she left the car at the station as though they'd caught a train.''

''You think it's still round here somewhere?''

''Yes—look at the facts.'' Webber drew his chair up to the table and Mrs. Thomas copied him. Really, he thought, she's brighter than half the incompetent plodders I had in the office, they'd all stopped listening to him as attentively as this years ago.

''It's a grubby little piece of antique pottery, not the sort of thing you steal unless you know it's valuable.''

''Have you found out what it's worth?''

''No, but more than I thought. I came back through Cambridge today and saw some people at the Fitzwilliam Museum. They wouldn't put a price on it but they say there can't be more than about twenty of them in the whole world so it's anyone's guess, but worth a lot, right?''

''Right,'' Mrs. Thomas cupped her chin in her hand but misjudged the edge of the table with her elbow and then delighted Webber by laughing at herself first.

''Silly cow, pissed again. Go on, love.''

Yes she was better than the office any day—worth cultivating.

''Mrs. Thomas . . .''

''Lizzie.''

''Lizzie then—you seem to have managed to get half of Flaxfield into the shop for the funeral but,'' and he held his finger firmly in the pool of beer and Guinness spilt when she had jogged the table, ''how many could have known it for what it was?''

''Adam Goodman,'' she said promptly, ''and that Mr. Trottwood, they knew. Doreen told me.''

''And the Vicar knew, he collects the stuff.''

She nodded. "Yes he knew, but I don't think it was him—not from talking to him."

"You can't leave him out, perhaps he's covering up."

"All right, that's three, who else?"

"Well the American, obviously."

"But he was trying to buy it."

"That could be covering up too—he might already have taken it. Did he have a briefcase or anything?"

Mrs. Thomas closed her eyes with concentration. "No," she said, "no, he didn't and he couldn't have hidden anything in that suit, it was too well cut—waisted—very posh. Goodman didn't have a bag either, nor the other one, Trottwood."

"Dr. Maguire did though, didn't he?"

"Yes he did—a carrier bag. I saw him with it when they phoned up for him. He had to see someone in the surgery." She fell silent and Webber wondered if perhaps after all he had overestimated her. To have a vicar and a doctor proposed within seconds as possible suspects might be more than she could contemplate objectively.

"That Maguire is a cocky little bugger," she said. "He likes antiques too. Doreen said he was always trying to buy things on the cheap. Anyone else?"

"There was a sort of little dealer man from London. Mrs. Corder can't remember his name."

"Cabert," said Mrs. Thomas. "Eddie Cabert, it was stencilled in silver on his crash helmet. I saw it in the kitchen."

"Shall we have one for the road?" said Webber looking at her with affection.

As he ordered the drinks the young girls who had been giggling with Burnstead exchanged a secret look and, smoothing their skirts, sought the lavatory. He made a mental note to ask his new assistant why women always went to the lavatory in pairs.

"One Guinness and one pint," he said, back safely in the corner, "and then I'm going to bed—tomorrow I can start."

"Start where?"

"Might as well get the obvious one out of the way. I'll take a walk up to the Old Thatched House."

"Has Doreen mentioned expenses?" The suddenness of the question took him by surprise.

"There's no need."

"No of course she wouldn't. It's not that she hasn't thought of it, but she's a bit stingy." Only ingrained loyalty stopped her telling him her opinion of Doreen's funeral arrangements. "Don't worry I'll see to it. I'm not short of a few quid."

Webber smiled at her, liking her for the direct way she said what was in her mind. It was late and he was too hot and too tired to explain that he was doing what he wanted to do, that it was as much for himself as for her or Doreen or anyone else. What was it Lady Ormundham had said? "The secret is to let people help you."

"Let's leave it until we see what happens. I can't guarantee a Gower case every day you know. Tell me why you don't like Dr. Maguire, apart from being a cocky little bugger, I mean."

Mrs. Thomas thought carefully.

"He pretends to like people but he doesn't really. He's thinking of himself all the time, his fingernails are dirty and when he's drunk he tells his housekeeper too much."

A piercing shriek cut through the bar and the two girls who had been talking to Burnstead at the bar came in looking shaken and pale. Webber had half risen but Mrs. Thomas reassured him.

"Nothing serious. That Irish tinker's parked his horse and cart in the back yard. I gave her some crisps through the window of the lav. I expect she's stuck her head in looking for more."

Webber glanced round the bar craning his neck to check the tables not in his direct view.

"He's not here, supposed to be talking business with Doreen. Finding her feet a bit, only natural I suppose, poor little sod."

"I shouldn't worry. I have an idea Mrs. Corder knows how to take care of herself."

"I meant him. She says he's a runner, what's that?"

"A dealer of sorts—you run things from one shop to another, buy a bit, sell a bit. That's one thing our local copper did help with. I thought he'd know about young O'Shea and he did. Does the rounds with the cart, Suffolk mostly, no fixed address, sleeps rough perhaps, gets accused of pinching junk sometimes but he's well liked on the whole. Burnstead says he's quite bright—not bright enough to spot a Pew Group but then I wouldn't have been either. I wonder what she gave him for it."

"She won't say, I asked her. Not much, I'll bet, knowing her."

Seeing Webber's face with its puzzled smile and the unasked question in the blue eyes she added frankly, "We've never been really close. I don't like her much. Listen, before I forget, what did you think of him?" She nodded at the bar where Burnstead was soothing the girls and joking with the landlord.

"Burnstead? Average bright, there's another child on the way, that'll be three so he gives a hand here a couple of nights a week, why?"

"I just wondered. His wife cries a lot."

It didn't much matter, Webber decided, where she got her information from—the doctor's housekeeper most likely. It was the sort of stuff you never got from computers, anyway. With the comforting sound of Katie's departing hooves on the cobbled paving of the yard at the back, Mrs. Thomas finished her drink and decided that the coast was clear for a decorous return. Doreen might not feel like a chat but you never knew. She wanted handling with tact, that was all.

By the time Webber had unpacked his suitcases he was already looking forward to the comfortable bed and the day ahead of him. Yet it wasn't the Pew Group he thought of as the chatter of the last customers leaving the bar came through his open window. First he thought of his wife and her awful sister as he'd seen them earlier in the day surrounded by travel brochures and preparing cold bloodedly to inflict themselves upon an unsuspecting cruise liner for the winter. He fell asleep with a smile of pity for the other passengers. The cruise didn't enter his dreams. He was marrying Lady Ormundham in St. Peter's Flaxfield and Mrs. Thomas was the matron of honour.

CHAPTER 12

WEBBER WOKE BECAUSE someone was tapping on his bedroom door. It was the landlord to say that he was wanted on the telephone downstairs. He took the call in his dressing gown, the passage was filled with sunlight and smelled of stale beer and disinfectant.

"Webber here."

"It's Lizzie Thomas—look I've just bumped into Mrs. Clifton. Mr. Trottwood got some tranquillizers from Dr. Maguire yesterday. He's upset because the other one's gone."

"Adam Goodman's gone?"

"Yes."

"Did she say anything else?"

"Yes, plenty as usual but nothing else important for us."

Webber thanked her and promised to let her know the result of his visit. It would be silly to forego his breakfast, he thought, if Goodman had skipped there was no point in enquiring about him on an empty stomach.

At the Old Thatched House Betsey Trottwood sat alone at the breakfast table for the second morning running. Unlike Webber he wasn't hungry. Out of habit he spooned out some Swiss Muesli onto his plate adding some All Bran and four prunes. He always had four because that made the stones add up to Sailor which was nicer than Tinker or Tailor or even Soldier. Before he could take the first spoonful after adding the milk the shop bell rang as the door opened and Webber introduced himself. John Webber may have prided himself on looking and behaving untypically for a policeman, not overtall, mild and gentle in his manner, a nice smile and an apology for disturbing him which was obviously sincere. To Betsey he couldn't have looked more like a policeman if he'd come in on a horse and in uniform.

It took Webber some time to dispel the image but he did it. The breakfast cereal lay between them congealed into a soggy mess. He asked if he could help himself to a cup of coffee and poured one for Betsey who began to look less like crying.

"If he has made a fool of himself and taken it we might as well see if we can find him together don't you think? I've told you the truth you know, the enquiry is quite unofficial but suppose it gets out of hand?"

Betsey had been using the tranquillizers to protect himself from that precise possibility.

"You mean if he tries to sell it to someone and they get suspicious?"

"Something like that."

The shop bell announced the inopportune entrance of Miss Hislop in unseasonable lightweight tweed and a silk square scarf on her head. It was printed with tan horse bridles on a powder blue background.

"Good morning and isn't it a beautiful one? Goodness

what lovely things you do have! It's such ages since I was in last, quite lovely. May I just look round? I was only saying to Mr. Goodman the other day it was a treat I'd been promising myself for ages. He was telling me that you had one or two things I might like to look at.''

''I'm afraid Mr. Goodman is away at the moment, do you happen to know what he had in mind?''

Miss Hislop's eyes quartered the shop, registering the stock and the open door of the dining alcove with Webber finishing his coffee.

''Well I'm afraid I don't—not that it matters a bit. I can pop in anytime. My mother,'' she added informatively, ''had some beautiful antiques, I must tell you about them. One day when you're not so busy perhaps.'' She seemed about to ask a question but changed her mind.

''What do you want me to do?'' Betsey asked Webber when she'd gone.

''You said he'd taken the car?''

''Yes and about £200 from the float.''

''Can I see the note.''

Betsey handed him the few lines in Adam's handwriting.

''There are some things I must see to. Not sure how long I shall be away. Didn't want to worry you about them until you're perkier. Have taken cash for petrol etc. Take care. Yours A.''

''Perkier?''

''We had food poisoning—they seem to think it was something we had at the funeral.''

''What was Corder like?'' asked Webber.

''I never liked him, I didn't trust him either.''

''Bit of a crook?''

''It wouldn't surprise me—oh dear! you must think me very unpleasant to say that. It's quite different with Adam, you know. I suppose that's because I understand him. You haven't told me what we can do.''

"He's taken the car," said Webber. "Where would he go? You say you understand him so you tell me where you think he is."

"I think he's gone to London," said Betsey.

Gaylor W. Whitman, Jnr. told the taxi driver to drop him on the corner of Mount Street. The short walk to the Connaught would let him test the strength of his legs. The private clinic where he had been recovering from Mrs. Thomas's sandwiches had been expensive but restful. His wife's morbid fear of hospitals and infection had limited her attendance to one apprehensive bedside encounter but he had been forced to endure a good deal of her on the telephone. She was a child of the instrument and since the age of seven had used it like a pen. On their honeymoon she had once talked to her mother in California for two hours and fifty-three minutes. They had been in Florence at the time and it had caused them to miss a private visit to the Uffizi. On the whole she was reasonably acceptable on the telephone, she marshalled her facts and presented them logically in a low nasal hum. In live conversation when animated she had been compared to Concorde. Her last call had explained her position with precision. As his secretary, being precise had been one of her most impressive accomplishments in her role as the dragon guarding the entrance to his cave. Later as his wife he had found her breath too hot. Even during the honeymoon her professed obsession with English pottery of the eighteenth century had shown signs of waning.

Her voice came back to him as he covered the last few yards towards the hotel entrance, the paving stones striking hot through the soles of his shoes.

"Sure I'm sorry you're sick, so the best place for you is home."

"Right"—it was always prudent to begin with that. "But I may have to stay on for a few more days, shouldn't take long, the fact is I'd really hate to miss it."

Telephonic artist that she was, she had not then been so stupid as to point out the absurdity of destroying a marriage for the sake of a lump of clay and thus opening up an irrelevant side issue.

"We're booked on a flight to New York on Thursday, if you're not on it with me I shall phone Jerry Beilin when I get in." Jerry Beilin was the divorce lawyer who had taken such good care of the lady she had replaced. She had then given him the flight number on Pan American, the time of take off, the estimated time of arrival in New York and rung off.

Some of the old affection for her clear headed efficiency came back to him and he was grateful. It had needed her calm assessment of the seriousness of the situation to focus his thoughts and bring him to his senses.

"Did Mrs. Whitman get off all right?" he enquired tentatively at the reception desk.

"Oh yes Mr. Whitman and, let me see, yes, she left a message."

There was no note in the envelope, only the first class air ticket.

"Quite recovered I hope, sir?"

"Thank you yes, I'm very well now. No other messages?"

"No sir, I believe Mrs. Whitman took some calls for you. We didn't have your number, I think she felt you needed rest. But there is a gentleman waiting to see you in the bar, a Mr. Webber I think."

* * *

"God's honour," Mrs. Thomas assured the vicar and his wife as they stood in the doorway of the shop where she had darted out to waylay them.

"Not half an hour ago, all three of them in Doreen's car, Mr. Trottwood driving because she's never been far in it by herself and the Inspector in the back to save petrol I expect and p'raps he's not supposed to drive with his heart."

"Oh dear I am sorry," said Joan Coley, "I had no idea. Poor man and he looks so fit."

"Nothing serious," Mrs. Thomas assured her. "Dr. Maguire's not worried but he suggested retiring a bit earlier. Lucky for us isn't it? And a lovely man. Good morning Miss Hislop, you're looking better, girl, I must say. She wouldn't touch the doctor's pills," she informed the other two as Miss Hislop loped towards them, "charcoal biscuits and boiled water."

The thought of refreshments came happily to Mrs. Thomas and with a cursory glance up and down the street to see if she could enlarge her audience she satisfied herself with the three she had and shepherded them into the shop.

"Of course," said the vicar sipping his coffee, "the fact that Major Goodman left the funeral in rather an odd manner doesn't prove that he stole it. He might have a perfectly innocent reason for acting so suspiciously."

"Be nice to know what it was though, wouldn't it?" said Mrs. Thomas offering round a plate of chocolate biscuits which, being obviously not home-made, were accepted by them all.

"Did the Inspector say how long they expected to be away?" asked the vicar.

Mrs. Thomas shook her head happily, stretching her little short legs out in front of her. How much nicer it all was than her small dark house in Cardiff where the rows with her friends and neighbours had long ago settled into a passionless ritual as devoid of fun and novelty for them as they were for her.

"I might open a bit earlier in the mornings," she said to no one in particular. "Seems a shame to have to wait until ten, especially since the opposition is closed."

"I suppose," said Joan Coley, "that Mr. Trottwood might best know where to look for him. I simply can't believe," she said more loudly and firmly as she brushed a crumb of chocolate into a brown streak on her skirt, "that Major Goodman would do such a stupid thing."

"Mr. Trottwood thinks he could," said Mrs. Thomas gently.

"So do I," said Miss Hislop. She said it with such sincerity that the others waited with interest for her to supply the reason for her conviction but they were disappointed for she concentrated on her coffee and did not enlarge on her statement. Mrs. Thomas regarded her with interest. Some sources of information, like the doctor's housekeeper, were like taps to be turned on without effort. Others, like Miss Hislop, needed a more subtle approach. The time was not now, but she made a mental note to cultivate Miss Hislop's friendship.

In the bar of the Connaught Hotel, Webber had introduced himself and explained his business and his unofficial status, sipping his ice cold lager appreciatively. Gaylord heard him out without interrupting.

"And you think he'll try and sell it to me," he said when Webber had finished.

"I'm assuming that he's got it," said Webber. "In fact I'm pretty certain he has. I still have a lot of contacts in the force. I've checked him out and he's got a record, quite a list. Fraud—he's not entitled to Major of course—receiving, offences against minors—if you can call boys of eighteen minors anymore—a small time con man, he was always in debt to bookmakers, he's done some time, two months for stealing from a friend's antique shop. Not this friend, Trottwood seems to have been a good influence on him, but the potential's there all right.''

''What makes you think he would offer it to me?''

Webber's pale blue eyes smiled apologetically. ''He's obviously a bad judge of character or he wouldn't have got himself in so much previous trouble.'' The quiet preamble was calculated to sugar the pill. ''He would probably think it out something like this. It's too hot to offer openly to the usual legitimate markets. Sale-rooms are out, they get their best prices by advertising widely, especially a piece like that. Dealers? Well he probably knows a few crooked ones but they would only give him a fraction of what it's worth. Of course he may have been so pressed for money that he would have taken anything for it but collectors are his best bet. Collectors—some collectors—can be quite ruthless in their pursuit of a rare item. His ideal choice I imagine would be a very rich collector. An American who was leaving the country perhaps and wouldn't ask any questions.''

''Mrs. Corder wouldn't sell it to me,'' said Gaylord after a long pause. ''Would you know why that was?''

''I should think she wanted to find out how much it was worth.''

''There is no question about her own entitlement to it?'' If he was submitting to questions he felt justified in asking some of his own.

''No, none whatever, she bought it from an Irish tinker with a horse and cart and he bought if from a junk stall at a church fête.''

Gaylord nodded sadly. "I was going back to the States but I'll stop here for a while, maybe you'll come up with something."

"This is where I'm staying," said Webber, giving him a small card which said "Glockemara Hotel, Notting Hill Gate, restaurant open to non-residents."

"How are things at Glockemara?" asked Gaylord with a brave attempt at humour he didn't feel.

"It's small but clean," said Webber. "Perhaps he's tried to contact you and failed. He might try again. You could get me there, they take messages."

For a long time after Webber had gone Gaylord sat thinking earnestly and he hoped constructively. Then he took the lift to his suite and placed a call to his wife in New York.

Chapter 13

Miss Hislop was not a foolish woman; simple perhaps, but not simple minded. She had never been a beauty, having been advised by her mother as a child not to expect it. Now in the summer of her thirty-eighth year she did not regard herself as that traditional figure, the casually pitied village spinster, and only rarely was she sorry for herself. Through the revolution of paperback publishing and with an intelligence that had been sadly wasted she had accurately diagnosed her condition and had not yet abandoned all hope of effecting a cure. Her faith, both in Freud and the Church, remained unshaken. She saw nothing wrong in praying for sex, and although she was well aware that her more specific supplications might well be gently disregarded as unreasonable, she occasionally allowed herself the luxury of mentioning Michael Sabini.

Mrs. Thomas had cultivated the art of listening with patience and intelligence but although Miss Hislop had been flattered by her attention and genuinely pleased to have her company on the evenings when Mrs. Thomas had called after closing the shop for the day, she had proved difficult to envelop in a neighbourly cocoon of intimate gossip. On her last visit she had discovered among Miss Hislop's modest collection of records a Victor Sylvester Latin American selection in strict tempo. In strict tempo she had volunteered to initiate Miss Hislop into the intricacies of the Tango and, although they were not ideally matched, Miss Hislop had been delighted. The record, she confessed, had been among those provided by Constable Burnstead who supplied the music for the occasional dances at the village hall and she had been so incensed at her inelegant showing when Mr. Sabini had asked her to dance *Jealousy* with him that she had surreptitiously removed it at the end of the Jubilee Ball in a fit of frustration and shame.

"Only temporarily of course. I thought I might master the basic steps at home but it was more difficult than I had imagined I'm afraid, so I'm really most grateful."

"She's mad about the curate," Mrs. Thomas reported to Webber on the telephone, "but I couldn't get a word out of her about Goodman. She knows something though, I'm certain. How's Doreen?"

"She seems fine, she's out a good deal with Jimmy Trottwood. It's odd but so far there's been no sighting anywhere. They're covering ground I wouldn't know about, and would have taken me weeks of slog. They started up here you know, Goodman and Jimmy Trottwood, had a stall in Portobello market, so Jimmy's been taking her round the old haunts. To be honest I can't think why she insisted on coming. I'm surprised she can leave the shop for so long."

"She's there because she doesn't trust anyone and if there's a chance of that Pew Group turning up she wants to be on the spot—simple."

"Ah!"

"Tell her I've sold two button hooks and a spinning wheel since I spoke to her, that's all she ever wants to know about. I can't get a word out of her about your end."

"I think she's a bit tired," said Webber. "She had a fairly confusing evening in a club called The Gay Parrot; she's probably a bit shy about telling you."

"She's never told me anything much but I manage. I've had that Irish boy lurking around after her most days. Wants to know when she's coming back, business he says, but he's randy that's all. Pretty boy, but what's the good of a tinker in a nice antique business? How've you been doing?"

"It's disappointing, Lizzie. Whitman was my best bet and there's not a flicker there, not yet anyway. I'll get back to him but Goodman should have surfaced by now if he's going to. I thought he might have tried the British Museum or the Victoria and Albert but he hasn't. There's a few more possibles. It takes time but I'll let you know. How're the legs?"

"They'll be all right when the Tango dies down."

"Keep at it, we might set up a detective agency one day."

"Lovely! In Flaxfield?"

"Not in London certainly, they can stuff it."

"At least you didn't have to go to America or South Africa."

Webber grinned through the grubby glass doors of the telephone box across the entrance hall of the Glockemara which the staff had been bullied into calling the foyer.

"You mean I should have searched Maguire's surgery first. Is that what you're trying to tell me?"

"No, I think Lily Clifton would have found it by now. I was only thinking—oh help! there's three American women outside in tartan trouser suits and God save us they're coming in."

"I'll tell Doreen business is looking up," said Webber.

The Glockemara did a good breakfast and they had taken to using it to meet and compare notes of the previous day. On Friday Webber told them that the trail was dead, had never been alive.

"It's my fault," said Betsey. "I was certain he'd come to London, he always does when he's in a mess." He absent-mindedly helped himself to another prune.

On that Friday Webber was going to see a dealer who specialized in fine rare pottery and porcelain. Tomorrow Betsey was to visit Portobello Road market. There was no point in going there on a Friday when it would be half closed.

"So we're taking the day off," he told Webber. "I thought about getting a hair cut," he added with a touch of defiance, "but I've had a better idea. She needs cheering up," he said, nodding at Doreen, "so we're going shopping. It does wonders sometimes. Shoes I think."

Doreen avoided Webber's eyes and concentrated on Betsey's plate.

"Five stones—that's nice. That comes to Rich Man."

At both the British Museum and the Victoria and Albert they had suggested Webber should contact Inicums. If a Pew Group was wandering around on the open market then it was to Inicums it was most likely to find its way.

"It would be nice to think so." Mr. Inicum waved Webber to an armchair in his overcrowded office. The table which served as Mr. Inicum's desk was untidily piled with books. If it weren't for the general atmosphere of learned chaos, Webber thought, Mr. Inicum might well have been a bank manager interviewing a client. Quietly dressed in a grey suit, almost bald, his sensitive face proclaimed success and cautious courtesy. It was the hint of caution in his manner that made Webber decide not to mention that he had retired. There was a suggestion of authority in the man that might not have responded to the unofficial approach. He needed to be outranked.

"You will appreciate I'm sure, Inspector, that in a house like Inicum's we regard a lot of our information as being of a privileged nature."

Webber's heart thumped—Inicum knew something!

"We accept that from the Church," his eyes were unblinking, his voice louder to convey a warning. "From everyone else we expect the fullest cooperation. That helps us," he continued a shade more mildly, "to protect your interests from the beginning. But I'm afraid that the privileged nature of anything you may know in this matter—anything at all—remains in our domain not in yours."

To Webber's surprise Inicum nodded agreement quite brightly and with no sign of resentment. On the contrary he gave every appearance of a man who has been given a licence to enjoy himself.

"In fact I was approached some time ago to see if I would be interested in buying a Pew Group."

"Do you happen to know his name—this person who approached you?" Webber asked as casually as he could.

"Oh yes, oh yes indeed." Mr. Inicum brought the tips of his fingers delicately together. "He was a dealer, he'd been in before from time to time. He called himself Matthews but I happen to know that it wasn't his real name."

Webber waited.

"It's an odd little story," said Inicum. "Can I offer you a glass of sherry, Inspector?"

He poured the wine as carefully as he chose his words to make sure that Webber appreciated them equally.

"He ran a small antique business with his wife in the Fulham Road—rather a striking looking woman, she came in with him once."

"His wife?"

"She was most certainly introduced as Mrs. Matthews."

"Forgive me," said Webber, "but if he had his own business as an outlet why would he prefer to sell to another dealer?"

"A small shop in Fulham," said Inicum mildly as he sipped his sherry, "could hardly command the prices I am prepared to pay for quality and rarity."

"I see, of course, please go on."

"I can look up my files but I suppose I must have bought two or three quite nice pieces from him from time to time, a group of Chelsea dancers I seem to remember. Red anchor mark."

"But you didn't buy the Pew Group?"

"Unfortunately it was not a direct offer—an exploratory approach. It's not uncommon with very rare pieces, you understand. People put out feelers, you know the sort of thing. 'It's not actually in my possession yet but I might be able to tempt the owner, etc.' The old story—shopping around. He spent a lot of his time away from Fulham travelling around looking for stock he told me."

"You said that you happened to know Matthews wasn't his real name."

"Yes—I must tell you, Inspector, that I have no reason to doubt Mr. Matthews' honesty. In every case where I have bought from him he has produced irreproachable evidence of provenance and entitlement of ownership. With us it has to be like that, you understand."

Webber remembered the impressive display of the coats of arms on the shop window announcing that Inicums was By Appointment to their royal holders.

"So the false name?"

"Oh very simple. I've read about such cases but never had first hand experience of one before. I had been asked down to the country to value a rather important collection. I drove down with Mrs. Inicum, she quite enjoys such expeditions, she always accompanies me, and she's helpful with notes and so on. My secretary could manage just as well but my wife looks forward to the change she says."

Webber had interviewed pedants before and knew when not to interrupt however much he longed to. People had their own rhythm, you waited for them.

"On our way back," Inicum continued, "we passed through a rather pleasant country town and stopped to have a look round an antique shop which had caught my eye. To my surprise the first person I saw upon entering was our Fulham friend Mr. Matthews."

Webber had a mental picture of the two of them, Inicum and his wife making the bell jangle as they opened the door of the Old Thatched House and confronted Adam Goodman and Betsey.

"I remember thinking that he might believe I was poaching on one of his country contacts. However before I could reassure him he spoke to me first. I can remember almost exactly what he said. He said, 'Good afternoon, I don't think we've met. My name is Rupert Corder and this is Mrs. Corder. Can we help you?' "

While Webber was adjusting to this surprising revelation, Inicum replenished their glasses.

"But on his last visit to you here," said Webber, "I mean surely that was after your country meeting wasn't it?"

"Oh yes indeed, quite some time after that."

"And did he refer to it in any way?"

"Absolutely not!" The sherry and the fascination of his own story had given Inicum the air of an excited schoolboy. He leaned forward, his palms pressed together and trapped between his knees.

"No, he was announced as Mr. Matthews as before and never said a word about the country!"

"I take it he showed you a Polaroid photograph of the Pew Group?"

"Yes, how clever of you, yes he did."

"Did you make him an offer for it?"

Some of Inicum's schoolboy enthusiasm faded to be replaced by his more customary caution.

"No, that would not have done at all—I told you he was shopping around, testing the market. I showed interest of course, that was quite proper and if, as I hope, he brings it in for a serious discussion, I shall do my best to buy it providing of course he can prove title to it."

"How much is it worth?" asked Webber but the House of Inicum appeared not to hear and discovered work to be done.

"Rather fun though, don't you think?" he said as he walked with Webber through the assembled treasures of the shop to the street door. "Matthews in town and Corder in the country, rather fun."

Webber thought he sounded wistful.

CHAPTER 14

SHEILA ORMUNDHAM AND John Webber sat on the corner of the terrace which would remain longest in shade until the sun drove it away in the mid afternoon.

"And you think she's no idea at all?"

"No I'm sure not. I even mentioned antique shops in the Fulham Road but she didn't turn a hair. I'll give him his due, he seems to have worked it all out very neatly. Long business trips away from Flaxfield, 'traveling around,' so of course she could never be sure quite where he was until he chose to phone her and she was tied to the shop here."

"While he was leading a double life in London."

"That's right—Mr. and Mrs. Matthews."

"But *she* knew—the Fulham Road one, I mean?"

"Oh yes, he couldn't have dove-tailed it so well without her knowing; the summer holidays with Doreen in Spain and so on."

"And she accepted all that?"

"Yes completely, she seemed very philosophical about the whole set up."

"So she's not likely to come charging down to Flaxfield and claiming half the stock of Corder's or anything dramatic like that?"

He moved his chair out of the sun into the shrinking shade.

"No, on the contrary, her main concern seemed to be that I might break the story to Doreen Corder. I got the impression that he'd seen to it that she was very well set up. She seems quite content to leave things undisturbed. They weren't married so there's no question of bigamy."

"It was quite a risk wasn't it? Two shops, two women?"

"It's not unknown. Perhaps Fulham Road was less inhibited than Flaxfield and it must have been useful for Matthews to sell things Corder had bought dishonestly. Did your husband ever sell him any Chelsea porcelain—or wouldn't you remember?"

She made a quick irritated gesture. "No, of course I can't remember. I knew Corder was a creep but I was a shy little mouse then. George was too trusting, a fool sometimes. Doreen Corder must be a bit dim too, don't you think? Unless she did find out and murdered him."

"Yes, I thought of that, but she didn't. You get a feeling about people," he explained modestly, "it's experience, I suppose. No she never had a clue about him. It's not a bad story though is it?"

"You're very good value. Gossip of the very highest quality."

"It works both ways, there's no one else I could tell."

"You're not going to say anything?"

"I'm supposed to be the good neighbour and helping. That news could hardly be welcome."

"And if she finds out?"

"Then I shall get good marks for discretion—at least I hope I shall. In any case it has no bearing on the real problem. Corder was dead and buried before the Pew Group disappeared, there's no possible connection."

Sometimes, Webber thought, it was difficult to know what was in her mind when she suddenly turned away as she did now. Did she sometimes catch an expression in his face that reminded her of his brother? People used to think them alike when they were boys. Would she think it such good value if he had chosen to ask her questions about DAVID?

"We didn't tell anyone but we hoped we were going to marry." Had that been an invitation, a form of permission to discuss it with her openly?

He found himself quite unable to do that, and curiously reticent about informing her that his wife and her horrible sister had inflicted themselves on an unsuspecting world cruise.

"The real problem? You mean the mystery of the vanishing Mr. Goodman?"

"Perhaps I was right to get out of the force. It's very shaming, you know. I was rather looking forward to showing off. It didn't seem too complicated; motive, opportunity, a tidy little record and just cracked enough to think he could pinch it and flog it himself. The American should have been the obvious answer but Goodman hasn't been near him. If he is holed up in London then it's somewhere he's never been with his friend Trottwood."

Soon the last of the shade would have gone leaving the terrace in the full light of the sun until it set into Henworth Woods.

"I wondered if you might care to come for a drive one

evening?'' he said. "Not far, a meal perhaps, we might find something in the Good Food Guide.''

In the car as he drove away he acknowledged that at least she had refused beautifully. Marriage to the old man had certainly given her grace. Perhaps it was too early to expect favour. The sun filtered through the thick overhanging trees of the drive and splashed gently on the windscreen. A cruise: his wife would never see anything as beautiful as this, even if she escaped an upset stomach and got ashore. Some ships had a poor record for food poisoning. She might goad her sister beyond endurance and get pushed overboard. Odd, too, how you never seemed to read of icebergs anymore. At the end of the drive a ruined Victorian lodge marked the entrance to the estate and the flow of traffic on the main road marked the end of his pleasant reverie.

He slipped into the stream heading for Flaxfield aware that he was no further advanced in a single significant fact. Adam Goodman had vanished and the Pew Group might never have existed. In his office at Ipswich the case would have been filed with a dozen others. A few computers across the country would have noted the facts without enthusiasm and he would already have started on something else. Only once had a computer surprised him, when it had unforgivably suggested that he might have taken a bribe. It had failed to provide any proof but it had been an added factor in his mind when he had considered Maguire's advice to retire early on medical grounds.

"Her tango is improving," reported Mrs. Thomas over her Guinness, "but her rumba is a shambles. I've ordered new stockings. Fair play—you can't say it wasn't worth it.''

Webber looked across the crowded bar to where Constable Burnstead was decorously pulling pints of golden bitter and smiling shyly at a girl in a print frock and plastic daisy earrings.

"She might be making the whole thing up, a frustrated spinster, it does happen, they're always the first to shout rape."

Mrs. Thomas pursed her lips judicially, savouring the double pleasure of the Guinness and her supporting evidence which had yet to come.

"She may well be frustrated but she wasn't complaining, she came out with it as natural as pouring a cup of tea, just casual and interested. Well—a bit excited perhaps—yes a bit, but no more than when she showed me her water colours."

Webber remembered some magazines they'd raided from a book shop in Cambridge. They had been shared out fairly among his men for Christmas.

"Water colours?"

She wasn't quite sure how much levity was allowed in a professional report, and since she was determined to show him that she was taking the investigation seriously she kept her face solemn but couldn't do much about her eyes.

"That's how it started. She went into Henworth Woods to sketch rabbits by moonlight. You have to keep very quiet for that or they won't come near you."

"Rabbits," he repeated evenly.

"She's doing it from a book, *How to Draw Bunnies*."

"And?"

"No bunnies; and no wonder with all that going on. About twenty kids she said, boys and girls, mostly teenagers but one or two about Burnstead's age, farm boys, the girls from the Co-op and some of the big boys in the choir, stark naked and at it like ferrets. She says Burnstead was obviously the leader of the pack."

"She didn't confront them?"

"She says she was too interested."

"That has a ring of truth but it's still only her word."

"Dr. Maguire has treated seventeen cases of minor infection over the last two years."

"Gonorrhoea?"

"Mostly thorns turned nasty, bums, backs and feet, nearly all girls, although some of the boys got bad feet."

"Kids go barefoot more than they used to, especially in a heatwave like this."

"Last summer was wet."

"A judge would tell a jury it wasn't good enough. You could go for an innocent walk—a picnic even."

"Not often at two in the morning."

"A time check is more impressive evidence I agree. May I ask how you got it?"

"Certainly, Marcia Evans, one of the Co-op girls—the fat one thank God—turned up at Dr. Maguire's at a quarter to three one morning."

"To take a thorn out!"

"No, to get a gin trap off her arse. Burnstead brought her, he 'found her in some distress' he said. She claims she was spending a penny. Took two of them using a tyre lever. Bad luck wasn't it, poor dab! Must have been thousands to one."

Mrs. Thomas met his eye unflinchingly and Webber was glad to refill their glasses as an excuse to avoid her studied control. Miss Hislop's unfettered imagination was one thing, clandestine operations to free fettered buttocks forced him to see Burnstead in a new light as he received his drinks and carried them back to the corner table.

"Gin traps are illegal," Mrs. Thomas said comfortably, "you'd only get them off the beaten track. Henworth Woods say."

"Was it followed up at all?"

"Burnstead said he'd report it."

"You got this from Mrs. Clifton, of course."

"From Lily, that's right."

"Any more?"

"Mrs. Burnstead knows there's something going on. Stayed behind after the Mothers' Union and cried to Joan Coley. He says he's out late on duty sometimes—has to be."

"And she doesn't believe him."

"No, and neither do you now any more than I do. The boy's all right, just a randy little bugger that's all, that's where all your Suffolk witches started, bet you anything."

"Lizzie, you have done very well. I'm not quite sure if it helps us but it's a bloody good story!"

Gin traps and orgies, but no Goodman and no Pew Group.

Mrs. Thomas's breasts swelled like the champion pigeon on the wall behind her.

"I think there's more to come from Mary Hislop yet—I never know if she's holding back or hiding something. Yet she seems so open—funny woman—she's a bit like a bran tub, you feel you might uncover something."

"Worth another rummage perhaps?"

"Oh yes," she drew proudly on her glass, conscious that she had not overestimated her natural talents and was deserving of his praise. To her surprise she suddenly realized that the outcome of her efforts was not as important to her as that sign of approbation from him. She wished very much that her clever sister in London could see her as she was now, the respected confidant of a famous detective, an active undercover agent in one of his most baffling cases. The most successful private detective agency in East Anglia —no, bugger it—in England.

128

In imagination she sat by his side in a speeding car pursuing a desperate Adam Goodman. Knocking dustbins flying and swirling up the scattered paper in their slipstream. Ignoring her legs she flung herself from wall on to the top of the cornered car. She survived booby trap bombs to be hurled across, landing safely into Webber's waiting arms with his blue eyes not six inches from her own.

Unaware of the closeness of their collaboration he sipped his beer. When he did turn to look at her he was so startled at the intensity of her gaze he found himself winking in embarrassed self defence.

God love him, she thought, another Guinness and I'd give him a kiss for that.

Dr. Maguire, far from being embarrassed or angry at Webber's knowledge of his patients' frailties, seemed to accept it as inevitable.

"I should have sacked her years ago, John, but where the hell can you find anyone better for the money I pay her? You can't, so I put up with the old cow and her gossip."

"But the Burnstead circus is true—not gossip?"

"Oh it's true enough, although the ladies seem to have given it the full dramatic value. Kids playing about, those woods have been full of it for years, I dare say. Burnstead seems to have organized it a bit more than most that's all."

Webber remembered his own solitary walks in Henworth Woods as a boy. The girls nowadays seemed less elusive than in his day. Perhaps they were all on the pill.

"The pill makes it easier, there's no doubt of that." Maguire poured a drink for Webber and topped up his own glass. "You know there's room for a fascinating field-study there, John. The effects of promiscuous sex on the body metabolism. Of course they're all young but the fact is not one of them caught the 'flu in last year's epidemic.''

"Was Adam Goodman ever part of these romps, do you know?''

"Ah! your missing suspect—not his taste at all now, was it? That's an odd sort of question from an old policeman, John!''

"He might have formed a splinter group,'' said Webber with dignity. "The thing is,'' he added defending his position, "I'm beginning to wonder if there might not be some other reason for Goodman's disappearance.''

"Blackmail?''

"There's always a danger with that combination. The highly respectable front, ex-army major. You know he never openly admitted his relationship with Trottwood? It was supposed to be purely a business partnership.''

Maguire nodded. "There was some talk about a Henworth choirboy, not one of Burnstead's lot, his choirboys were straight as dies both of them. But there's a younger kid out there, about fourteen, a born tart. I wouldn't even have him in the consulting room alone, not without his mother I wouldn't.''

"Was there anything in it?''

"Probably—it never became general gossip, hushed up, I seem to remember—not even the Clifton got hold of it for once, so it must have been pretty vague. You'll stay to dinner, John?''

When Webber hesitated Maguire beamed expansively holding his arms wide without spilling his drink. "Come on now. I can offer you delicious duckling and bread-and-butter pudding with eggs and cream, everything they say you shouldn't have and I say you should! What splendid temptation, blessed by a good medical brain.'' He placed a persuasive arm round Webber's shoulder. ''You shall have the best claret in Suffolk and I shall be wildly indiscreet with my gossip. Who knows? between us, we may even solve your lovely mystery for you!''

CHAPTER 15

GAYLORD W. WHITMAN Jnr. ended the conversation with his wife in New York with disappointment and relief. He had telephoned her to find out who had been trying to contact him at the Connaught while he was recovering in the clinic. Early on when she heard his voice she had assumed that he was clumsily attempting a reconciliation and had been touchingly pleased to assume her role as efficient guardian of his affairs. She listed all his calls at the Connaught from memory and with precision. None of them had been from Adam Goodman and that was disappointing. When it had dawned on her that this was the sole reason for his call she had been equally precise in reiterating in detail the reasons for the failure of their marriage and her irrevocable intention of proceeding with the divorce. And that was a relief.

As the weekend drew nearer Joan Coley cried quietly into some over-ambitious recipe books and William came very near to tears over the composition of his Sunday sermon.

"And now abideth faith, hope, charity, these three"; and on Saturday morning when Eddie Cabert decided to telephone Gaylord Whitman at the Connaught Hotel he did so simply as a matter of expediency; part of a calculated set routine. Convinced that the American had bought the Pew Group from Doreen, it made sense to pretend that he bore him no grudge, that he was happy to congratulate him on his rare acquisition, and looked forward to helping him again in the future. He used the telephone reserved for the stall holders in his section of Portobello market.

Portobello: the largest street market for genuine antiques in the world. The first foothold for experts, the last refuge for failed fools, and between them a marvellous microcosm of success and failure, a treasure trove of astonishing bargains and the last burial ground of elephants with plastic tusks. A mediaeval reincarnation.

As Eddie listened to Whitman he soon discovered that his little obsequious routing was quite inappropriate. He hadn't bought it after all. It was missing and so was Adam Goodman.

"This guy Goodman, what's he like?"

Eddie judged people by their usefulness not by their moral standards. When Adam had been in Portobello he'd had an eye for quality but no idea of prices.

"He's O.K. I used to buy rather well from him."

"Eddie, I want that group, you know that."

"Yes I know that."

"O.K. Keep in touch, I'm staying over for a while."

"Oh, Mr. Whitman! Just a minute! I seem to remember you telling me that Mrs. Whitman collected glass paintings. Well I'll tell you what I have got. I've just found . . ."

"Forget it!" said Gaylord firmly and hung up.

Eddie left the telephone and pushed his way past the tourists, early bargain hunters who were already too late, and walked slowly back to the little stall he rented every Saturday. It measured four feet six inches by five feet ten and a half inches. He paid rent but not income tax or VAT. All around him in the hot, bright sunshine the bemused tourists shuffled and hovered around the stalls like wasps drugged and trapped by highly coloured sticky cakes. To have hooked a big fish like the Pew Group and then to be told that some idiot had let it slip out of the net saddened and angered him. Anger was a luxury he never allowed himself in business. It was unproductive, he had seen people lose good deals through lack of self control and catharsis was a poor exchange for profit.

Goodman might just be stupid enough to try and find a buyer through one of his old contacts. It wasn't very likely but it was possible. Eddie had a good chance of finding out. His private intelligence system was the best in the market. He looked at the woman who had been guarding his stall without enthusiasm. She had attached herself to him a long time ago with an unpaid doglike devotion, and the more unloved she was the more indispensable she had made herself. Some people said she had been a school teacher, others thought she had a small allowance. She could have been 35 or 55, it was impossible to guess and very few bothered to do so. For Eddie she ran errands and delivered parcels, she loved choc-ices and she loved Eddie. She knew everyone in the market and most of their prices. She could remember the names of foreign dealers and exactly what they had bought four years ago. She looked respectable and intelligent enough to visit the grandest antique shops in London and find out exactly what they were asking for anything which Eddie needed to price. Throughout Portobello market she was known as Mata Hari and although unloved, she was happier than most people.

Eddie looked at her mop of frizzed hair and her thick lensed glasses beaming a welcome as he approached. She was in a race against time with the last portion of a rapidly melting ice cream so that the happiness of her welcome was tinged with sticky anxiety. At least she no longer wore leather motorbike gear which in the early days she had mistakenly thought would please him.

"Do you remember a man called Goodman?" he asked, accepting the only chair on the stall as she stood for him.

"Adam Goodman? Yes he used to be in Collector's Corner with Jimmy Trottwood. They sold mixed stuff, brass, embroidery. He wasn't very nice, a terrible liar, said he'd been to Oxford. He was pinched for thieving and molesting boys at the Science Museum."

"That's him. I had some good buys there—ever see him since?"

"No, but it wouldn't surprise me if he is on the run. Jimmy Trottwood was down last Saturday asking about him. Why?"

Eddie gave her every bit of the story from the first wonderful moment when he had seen the Pew Group in Corder's window. He passionately believed in secrecy but he had never underrated Mata Hari's intelligence and loyalty. With the battle almost certainly lost you might as well arm your allies.

She listened carefully and folded the ice cream wrapping into a neat square, smoothing out all the wrinkles before she spoke.

"He must know roughly what it's worth and he's not going to get that down here or anything like it, and even if he'd been shopping around for contacts we'd have heard.

No; it won't come here, it's too hot. He might have tried one of the big boys, Inicum's perhaps, but I doubt it." She paused to explain patiently to a lady from Virginia that it was not Queen Victoria's friend who raided the armoury at Harper's Ferry.

"I'll tell you what will happen to it," she said when the Virginian lady had departed only half convinced. "Either it's gone for ever or the man will bring it out nice and clean and legitimate and then no dealer will get a sniff of it. It'll go to auction with a full page colour plate in the catalogue."

Eddie nodded miserably.

"And I was so near it," he said. He saw it again on the table in Corder's shop, not ten feet away as he stood on the pavement. "So bloody near."

Mrs. Thomas stood on the pavement sweeping it down vigorously with soapy water. Since the abortive London visit Doreen had remained sulky and apathetic, resenting her mother's presence and showing it. She wanted her to go home where she could no longer interfere with her life. It was intolerable that Doreen should be made to feel like a schoolgirl all over again. The resentment was mutual. The hard bristles of Mrs. Thomas's brush made a succession of satisfying sharp hissing stabs on the pavement stones, stippling her elastic stockings with a splash pattern like the walls of the dance halls of her youth. Resting on the handle of her broom she found herself unwilling to re-enter the shop. If Doreen went on spoiling things like this she'd pack up and leave, well perhaps not that, but it would serve her right—except, maddeningly, she knew it was exactly what Doreen wanted. The girl was flighty, lazy, mean, heartless and a little madam. God knows she'd done her best to help but you couldn't get through to her, not when you really wanted to know something, you couldn't. If the letter from the solicitor in Woodbridge had only come when Doreen was away on that fool's errand she could have steamed it open at leisure instead of having to deliver it to the moody little bitch and await her pleasure.

It was irritating, too, not to be able to use the telephone to speak to her sister in London when she wanted to, although if she were going to have to drag every little bit of news out of Doreen with a pair of pliers there would be precious little to report anyway. Thank God for Inspector Webber and that nice old poof Mr. Trottwood who had been kinder to Doreen than she deserved. She would stay outside on this wet pavement for hours if necessary, standing motionless, clutching the broom handle with tears pouring down her face until even Doreen would take pity on her, lead her poor mother gently back into the shop and tell her everything.

Her vow of silence did not include the vicar's cat, she considered, and she felt free to address Bunter as he sauntered towards her across the road.

"I've failed," she informed him dramatically. "Where did I go wrong?" she demanded as he strolled past her into the shop doorway. Once there, with sharp expert bursts, more efficient than any aerosol, he cocked a tail quivering with delight and sprayed the letter box and doormat to disperse the disgusting smell of soapy water.

"You dirty bugger! You've done it again!" she screamed at him as she reeled into the shop clutching the collar of her blouse across her nose.

Her impetus swept her into the kitchen where Doreen sat with the opened letter on the table in front of her. Instinct and common sense carried her round the table where she could embrace her daughter from behind. Instinct, because by the expression on Doreen's face she sensed that a breaking point had arrived, and common sense because if she was wrong in this assumption then at least she could read the letter over Doreen's shoulder.

Mrs. Thomas's high scream of rage sent Bunter flying back to the peace of the churchyard and carried clearly, although indistinctly, through the open window of the vicar's study where it served to bridge a silence which had fallen between William and his curate.

"Late for a curlew," murmured William.

Michael, whose ears were keener, let it pass, feeling that to comment on yet another example of human frailty could only serve to complicate the issue before them.

At the window William watched Bunter in the long grass stalking invisible prey with fierce, flat-eared concentration.

"And you believe it—you think it's true?"

Michael Sabini's face shone·with the innocence of pre-Raphaelite purity.

"Yes, yes I do, it—well it just *sounded* true. Some people one might doubt but I have never known—"

"Quite, quite," said the vicar. "I agree. You've told no one else?" Michael shook his head. "In the circumstances I did wonder about the Inspector or Dr. Maguire but of course the message was a personal one to you."

William paled. Purity and stupidity, he reflected, were not mutually exclusive. Bunter sprang too soon and the prize escaped.

"Quite right, at this stage it need go no further, I think. I must tell Mrs. Corder, of course. Joan says she has been very low and technically the Pew Group could still be regarded as her property."

The curate's eyes met his, trusting but troubled.

"Perhaps," said William, "we should now walk across

the road and see her together.'' His hand closed around Michael's arm with a grip that made him wince.

"You will keep the appointment," said William softly, "that is vital. But you will not mention it to Mrs. Corder, you will leave that entirely to me. Have I made that quite clear?''

And not until Michael nodded did William release his arm.

Mrs. Thomas emerged from the living quarters and met them in the shop.

"She's upset," she mouthed in a practised whisper, jabbing her finger towards her unseen daughter.

"So Mrs. Coley tells me," said William instinctively matching her tone. "The London visit, a failure, I know. However Mr. Sabini and I have some . . .''

Mrs. Thomas sensed the need for summary. "No! Worse! No money! Left her nothing!''

"But the will? Surely I understood—"

"Yes I know! in the *Will* yes— 'everything of which I die possessed,' but there's *nothing!* Only this," her circling arm encompassing the shop came dramatically to rest where Doreen was standing in the doorway.

"No need to whisper, Mam. Yes it's quite true, Mr. Coley, my husband left no money at all or to be accurate thirty pounds and fifty pence.''

"Mrs. Corder!—are you quite sure?''

"That's what the solicitor says. It's in the letter.''

William felt that it would be indelicate to refer to his own news immediately. Quite certainly the revelation of Doreen's impoverishment was going to make his appointed task more difficult but with faith and God's help he was determined to try, and God had never let him down so far. He must speak to Doreen privately, that was now essential. Meanwhile a few well chosen words before his curate could be judiciously comforting were in order.

"When bad things happen to us, we sometimes judge too quickly. It's so terribly easy to condemn. If we could hear poor Mr. Corder's explanation before that dreadful accident."

"It wasn't an accident," said Doreen. "I tripped him, I stuck my foot out and tripped him."

CHAPTER 16

"WE COULD GET pissed I suppose," said Doreen as Betsey was making the salad dressing for the modest lunch he was giving her.

"We could, but I should only zizz off in the shop or break something and you can imagine the fuss if—"

He broke off to dip his finger in the dressing and taste it. "More pepper? What do you think?"

The more she saw of him the more difficult she found him to understand. On the surface he was simple and apparently without guile and yet he was adept at evading questions he didn't want to answer, like a child who has discovered the power of clowning. She sulked and put up barriers; he crossed barriers and made people laugh so that they forgot the questions they'd asked him until he was ready to answer in his own time. She wondered what his mother had been like.

"That tastes all right to me," she said. "Has he done this before? going off—disappearing?"

She wasn't sure if his concentrated stare at the kitchen ceiling meant he was judging the salad dressing or his answer.

"Has he done this before," he repeated slowly and evenly. It was the tone of voice people used for party games at Christmas she thought. Like—is it loosely connected with transport?—not a question, more a consideration.

"Yes once or twice when he couldn't cope, more in the old days before we came down here. Depends on the drama; bets, boys or burglary."

Her face, he decided with approval, showed neither revulsion nor condemnation, simply puzzled interest. It pleased him that he had not over-estimated her. She was a late developer but not a fool. You could take a fool for a friend or even a lover but they were no good as confidants.

"So why do I stay with him?" he asked the question for her, licking the salad dressing off his finger. "That's easy, because the silly bastard needs me, that's why, and it works, too. London was a killer for him and we both knew it. Down here for the first time he's respected and he's never had that before. It means a lot to him." He smiled at her quickly. "He's very nice really, you'll like him when you get to know him better."

"But if he didn't take the Pew Group—Just supposing— then why did he go away?"

"Of course he took it, don't be silly, dear. I know it, you know it and so does the Inspector. Why do you think we've been chasing all over London? Listen, just because the vicar gets some sort of mysterious message about the Pew Group, what makes you so sure it didn't come from Adam? I'll bet it did, or he's behind it anyway. It sounds just like him, I know him so well. All right! I know you say you can't talk about it, but Adam took the Pew Group, I'm sure. It was all just too much for him. He probably put it in the folded carrier bag he took with him, we were going to buy some washing-up liquid on the way home. He's not very clever, I'm afraid. My guess is that it's just dawned on him that he can't possibly sell it safely so he's stuffing up poor old Coley with a pack of lies so that he can return it gracefully. He'll probably ask for a reward. Bugger it, I'm going to squeeze a clove of garlic in that. Business couldn't be worse, only those awful coach tours and they never buy anything, serve them right.''

He walked to the fridge in an exaggerated caricature of an American coach-load tourist lady, swinging open the door and producing the remains of his Sunday joint of beef.

"That, madam," said Betsey sweeping the joint on to the table with a flourish, "as your expert eye has already discerned, is a very rare piece indeed. Not only rare," he pressed down firmly on his wig with his left hand while the palm of the other hand pushed out towards his customer to prevent interruption, "but historic. It is the very joint of beef I had planned to serve to my partner, who is also my lover—yes the very meal, before he deserted me and left me as you see me now. Why! WHY! God knows the ways of a man madam! Who are we to judge—you and I—we are tools in their hands.''

He hadn't intended the double meaning and collapsed into a chair at the table where Doreen was already helpless with a handkerchief.

"Oh dear that's better! Oh I do love a giggle. I miss Peter Jones, especially the soft furnishings, it used to be lovely in my day.''

He watched Doreen fondly as she wiped her eyes and blew her nose.

"There you are you see," he said, patting her arm maternally, "better already and not a drop past your lips, still I don't see why we shouldn't have a beer, it'll bring out the best in the garlic. Rinse out the glasses with water first and they won't froth up." He watched her while he finished making the dressing. She's going to be like her mother when she's older, he thought. She can't stand her and she's going to be just like her. He himself liked Mrs. Thomas, as indeed did most people who had never shared a bathroom with her.

"Will your mother be all right on her own for a bit?"

"Yes now she's got her own way—for the time being anyway, says she's too shocked to travel for a bit."

"I don't wonder." He sipped the beer smiling disarmingly. "Did you really push him downstairs?"

"I didn't say push! I said I tripped him." If only she would laugh like that more often he decided it would do more for her than new shoes. "No of course I didn't. It was—oh I don't know—everything coming together I suppose. I wanted to shock them—so I just said it."

"Did they believe you?"

Doreen chuckled. "Mam did—it took us ten minutes to calm her down. I had to put ice cubes down her tits. She just stood there screaming and pointing at the staircase so I had to do something. She was all right when I said I was joking. Then the vicar said he wanted to talk to me so we left her with Mr. Sabini to dry out."

Betsey looked at her with genuine admiration. It was not his idea of a joke, but to create chaos like that as an instant antidote to relieve pent up feelings, and then as quickly to restore things to normality, was an achievement he could envy but knew he could never emulate. It was so much more positive than taking someone shopping.

"I see you're wearing the shoes."

She pushed her legs forward with toes pointed. "Of

course, they're beautiful. I shouldn't have let you do it. Fifty pounds! I didn't know anyone paid that for shoes.''

"They were meant," he said, "as part of an ensemble, dear, to cheer us both up. I'd forgotten that's all you can draw out of the Post Office at a time.''

"And did it cheer you up?"

"Oh dear, that meat doesn't look very appetizing, does it? Never mind, cover it with the salad. Yes, certainly it cheered me up. Clothes always help. I used to make things for my mother; dreadful they were but you couldn't argue with her she always got her own way. No taste at all. She was mad about Marina blue and it didn't help her veins a bit but she wouldn't listen, she used to look ghastly. I'd get her all dolled up, hat, ribbons, everything and we would go to all the society weddings. We'd queue up for hours outside the church or Caxton Hall, we were in all the newsreels. She looked like a maypole, and then you'd see this sad little thing in short trousers with her—that was me. She used to make her own confetti too, mean old cow, oh but we did laugh!''

"Did she know Adam?"

"Yes, couldn't stand him, she knew him for what he was, but then so did I—more salad?"

She shook her head. "Jimmy, do you think the vicar will really get it back—the Pew Group?"

"I hope so. God knows you could use the money.''

Doreen didn't comment on this. For once she found herself thinking with compassion of someone else's troubles.

"If you're so sure, who don't you ask him if he knows where Adam is too?"

He scraped the left-overs from her plate on to his own and carried them to the sink without answering.

"Don't you want him back?"

"I don't think I'll know until he walks through the door. I expect it will sort itself out. Anyway I won't worry about that today. I'll worry about it tomorrow. Wasn't she wonderful in 'Gone With the Wind'?"

"I never saw it," said Doreen. "At least I don't think I did."

"You mustn't blaspheme, dear."

With the meal over and the washing up shared, Doreen thanked him and prepared to leave. The thought of her mother in the shop depressed her. Since her hastily retracted confession of murder it had not been referred to again but Mrs. Thomas had taken to jumping visibly when spoken to and Doreen found it unsettling.

"Back to work?"

"Mam's better on her own. I'll walk for a bit now the sun's not so hot."

"Well keep to the path dear, you might meet a wolf in the woods."

"I'll worry about that tomorrow! You were sweet to give me lunch."

For a long time after she had gone Betsey sat in the shop letting his mind pick and probe at the days since Joseph's horse had nibbled the parsley in the window boxes and he had refused to buy the Pew Group, right down to today and the lunch with Doreen. He knew she wanted to talk and it had taken a great effort of will not to press her. He was proud of it but sad, because it tied his hands and he wanted to help her. She and Adam were alike, vulnerable and proud, frightened to trust in case they were cheated and lost something, like children. Perhaps she would change her mind. He hoped it wouldn't be too late. When Doreen had first told him that Rupert had left her nothing in the bank he had considered lending her some money until such time as she could make the shop support her. The caution he had always to remember with Adam overcame his natural generosity and he had said nothing.

Even Betsey had been shocked when his mother had left him all that money. Shocked at the amount and shocked at her duplicity through the years that had forced him to work for his living. Cutting up lengths of material by day, making her clothes and snipping up confetti by night while he paid rent to her for the privilege. Except that he had to admit that he had enjoyed every minute of it. When the headstone she had selected for herself was finally erected over her grave in Putney cemetery he had acknowledged her wisdom and Adam was told—and believed—that after they had bought and renovated the cottages in Flaxfield, it was the end of the money. After that the business would have to support them, and it had.

There was more of his mother in him than he knew.

The path in Henworth Woods which led to Joseph's cottage was barely a track, deep-rutted where the mud had baked solid since the drought. The cottage itself was a mess, long neglected, a relic of the days when the estate could afford gamekeepers. Shelia Ormundham could not even afford to pay Joseph for the odd jobs he helped with at the Hall. The cottage was all she could offer and it suited him well, inaccessible and remote, and shelter for Katie at the back.

From the tiny square of bedroom window Joseph watched Sheila Ormundham prop her stick against a tree some twenty yards away. She combed her hair, and deliberately leaving the stick, she picked her way among the worst of the ruts calling to the yellow labrador to follow her. In the months since Joseph had moved into the cottage her lameness had improved unbelievably. She was an unsentimental woman and put it down to the fact that she wanted to appear as attractive as possible when she was with him. The years between them seemed not to worry him in the slightest but they worried her. It was delightful to find not only that a beautiful young man could make love to her without a hint of condescension but with obvious enjoyment and for nothing more material than the use of a cottage little better than a stable. She worried because she couldn't understand it, but she had every intention of enjoying it for as long as she could. Anything which threatened to remove him from the estate and her life she was determined to counter if she could. She knew a bargain when she saw it.

"Lie quiet on the bed," Joseph told Doreen, "and I'll get rid of her."

"Perhaps she's only going for a walk," said Doreen in near desperation as she watched a good hour's delight being thrust unceremoniously into Joseph's jeans with only the butterflies to keep it company.

"Don't dress for God's sake," Joseph called over his shoulder, "the boards creak."

He was still tucking his shirt in as Sheila walked into the downstairs room.

"I'm sorry, I should have knocked."

"I've been on the roof, some of the tiles are loose. It's a good time to fix them before the rain."

What followed with bewildering speed was not at all what she had planned. The Hall was in desperate need of renovation but it was far better appointed for sexual adventures than the cottage. It was only now as her eyes became accustomed to the subdued light after the glare of the sunlight outside that she was delighted to observe his obvious excitement at their unexpected encounter.

The exact timing wasn't ideal for Joseph either but he was unprepared for her nurse's training and the speed with which it enabled her to get his jeans off. Neither was the decrepit horsehair sofa ideal for either of them, but the natural momentum of events at that moment made it seem infinitely more exciting than her double bed at the Hall. For Hannah, the yellow labrador, the boredom of a sedate walk through a wood full of heat-dazed rabbits was suddenly gloriously transformed. There was not only the joy and excitement of a wrestling match downstairs but, by bounding up the almost vertical staircase, there was another naked lady cowering on a bed and pretending to be frightened of her. It was difficult for a young happy dog to decide which was more fun, making quick darting nips at Doreen's ankles or tumbling back down the stairs where you could pounce with the full weight of your front paws on the beautiful bouncing butterflies, so full of life and energy and not a bit like the spoilsport rabbits who would not wake up to be chased.

All games must end and Hannah in her short life had already learned that humans tried and lost interest more quickly than she did. Inexplicable in their sudden changes of mood and temper, letting you romp with them one minute and seconds later putting you on a lead or even sending you to your basket. The trick was to judge the right moment to abandon them and fly for freedom.

Of the three females in Joseph's cottage that sunny, sexy day of midsummer only Hannah achieved complete happiness and satisfaction. Sheila's excitement was already yielding to discomfort and distraction. Hannah's hysteria in the bedroom had risen to the crescendo she usually reserved for postmen and when, goaded beyond endurance, Doreen's naked figure hurled itself down the staircase it was not upon Joseph and Sheila that she fell in fury but upon the fleeing form of Hannah who, with a muffled yelp of ecstasy, beat her to the door by inches. The yelp was muffled because she had one of Doreen's fifty pound shoes in her mouth.

CHAPTER 17

THE WEATHER SHOWED no signs of breaking. The ridge of high pressure centred itself over Flaxfield and extended its bounty beyond Lower Henworth as far as Scotland and most of northern Europe. Weather experts, appalled by its predictability, left cunning little loopholes in their forecasts, hinting at thunder and a change to conditions which, for the moment, they were bound on their honour not to disclose. In the north chantry chapel of St. Peter's the vicar was delivering a private report as calmly as he could.

"Lord something very odd has happened and I'd rather like your advice."

Webber sat on a tartan rug which Mrs. Thomas had spread in the shade of an oak tree whose roots went deep enough to defy the drought. The picnic was her idea. Both the Bull and Corders lacked privacy and Webber, she sensed, was depressed and needed encouragement to talk.

She put cold chicken and potato salad on a plate for him

151

with a hunk of crisp French bread and more butter than the police doctor had advised for a month. He spread all the butter inside the length of the bread and closed the two halves together in case his wife appeared from the bushes, remembering with relief that with luck she might be embroiled in street fighting in Greece. *Mrs Thomas* She watched him eat his food and enjoy it, delighted that he approved of her chocolate cake. They drank tinned lager agreeing that it was better than coffee.

"I thought Joan Coley would know," she said as she opened two more tins, "but she doesn't, and that's Gospel."

"How long was she with him?"

"Over two hours, first in the vicarage and then wandering round the churchyard."

"And you've no idea what they were talking about."

"If she thinks I believe they were discussing a headstone for Rupert she must be simple."

"She's not simple," said Webber.

"Oh no, I know that, not simple." She brushed some crumbs from her lap. "She gets daft ideas in her head, John."

The pleasure and comfort she took in Webber's company was spoiled for her. She could hardly be expected to disclose Doreen's confession of murder. True, she had retracted it almost at once and Webber was certainly a retired policeman, but she held back. The vicar was right, the girl was overwrought, lashing out and not caring who got hurt. Regretfully it was best forgotten. She was very lucky that only her mother and the church had witnessed her temporary derangement. That's what the vicar had said and he was right. Doreen was lucky, and she didn't deserve it. Whatever other words of comfort or wisdom he had imparted had

been given to Doreen alone during that long homily delivered first in his study and later, more maddeningly, in full
view but in the silent dumbshow of their earnest walk
around the churchyard. Not for the first time in her life had
Mrs. Thomas regretted her inability to lipread. Since that
mysterious talk with him Doreen's air of settled gloom and
evasiveness had driven her mother into a frustrated fever of
curiosity. First the solicitor and now the vicar. Mrs. Thomas
felt she was struggling to play a game where the players kept
changing the rules as they went along.

"What sort of daft ideas?" asked Webber.

Mrs. Thomas reluctantly abandoned Doreen's dramatic
outburst; luckily Doreen was not short of daft ideas.

"She thinks she can manage the shop on her own. Well
that's daft for a start, nothing in the bank and the best thing
in the shop stolen."

Webber grunted; a delicately disguised belch. Yesterday
Mrs. Thomas had seen him drive off in his car and he'd been
gone for most of the day. If he was going to tell her about it
she'd given him a quiet opportunity, someone had to play
fair sometime. She made a conscious effort not to wriggle
her bottom.

"The chicken was good, Lizzie."

Mrs. Thomas beamed. "Boiled with rib bones from
smoked bacon, you can get them for nothing. I let it cool in
the liquor. Don't tell that bloody doctor, he'll say I've
poisoned you. You quite like him, though, don't you?"

"I don't dislike him, but I'm not sure that I trust him
much."

"Lily Clifton says he's mad about antiques, been collecting them for years—dust traps she calls them." Her sudden enthusiasm had raised her to her knees, her eyes shining

153

like a dog eager to fetch its lead for a walk. Webber patted the rug gently and she was told to sit.

"Look Liz, it's not simple like that—yes of course Maguire could have taken it. As it happens I was in his surgery when he came back from the funeral. He had a shopping bag full of vegetables but he could easily have hidden it underneath. And where does that get us? Nowhere, Lizzie, that's where, because whoever's got it has found out by now that they can't sell it like a teapot, it's too important. You might just as well try and sell the Mona Lisa."

He found his pipe and tobacco and started to fill it, guessing her train of thought.

"The British Museum has one," he said, "and so does the Victoria and Albert Museum. The museum in Staffordshire where these Pew Groups were made hasn't even got one of them."

Mrs. Thomas attempted a revised estimate of Doreen's loss, and failed.

"That museum in Cambridge," he continued easing up the tobacco with a twig where he'd packed it too tightly, the Fitzwilliam, they've got more than anyone, about six I think. That's where I went again yesterday."

"How much is it worth?"

"They won't tell you—the dealers won't either. It depends who's buying it, that's as much as I could get—about the price anyway. But they did tell me something else. I've had a feeling about the Fitzwilliam, that's why I went back."

She waited until he succeeded in lighting the pipe.

"I was the second person they'd had asking about the current value of Pew Groups."

"Maguire!"

"No, it wasn't, but he made no secret about his identity and certainly the description fits."

"Adam Goodman."

"No, he said his name was William Coley and that he was the vicar of Flaxfield."

For William it was a busy and exciting time. The pleasantest part by far had been his visit to the Fitzwilliam Museum. True he had not been able to discover how much a Pew Group could be expected to fetch on the open market but there had been the joy of seeing the museum's collection again and comparing all six of them with the one he had glimpsed so tantalizingly in Corder's shop. They were all fine examples of course, world famous indeed, but not one of them was so superb as the one he had begun to think of as his own.

His visit to Archdeacon Gray had been, as he suspected it would be, a complete waste of time and petrol. Nevertheless it had been his duty to go. No one should say that he had not pursued every orthodox solution to a problem which was becoming more urgent with every week that passed. St. Peter's bells could no longer be rung; there had been no sound from the organ since the hymns at Rupert Corder's funeral service, and Mrs. Willow had received a glancing blow on the wrist from a fragment of rotten wood no bigger than an acorn which she was now describing as a beam. She wore her arm in a sling and it had caused havoc with the rota for flower arranging.

The Archdeacon had not been persuaded to champion the cause of St. Peter's above those of rival claimants. He had prepared himself with pleasure for some fairly vicious infighting and was surprised and disappointed by William's philosophical, even jovial, acceptance of his judgment. It had denied him the pleasure of Christian consolation and confirmed his opinion of Flaxfield's vicar as a potential trouble maker, given to exaggeration and secrecy. The likeliest explanation was that he was a communist. William's opinion of the Archdeacon he confided only to Joan and to God.

"Lord, no one knows better than you that the true path is not easy to find, it was a point I was trying to make in my sermon on crosswords if you remember. Well now, I begin to see that if Archdeacon Gray is a clue, then he is no longer simply a stubborn old fool but a stubborn old fool with a purpose, serving your will as so many of us must do without knowing why but essential to the ultimate solution."

William's gift was that he had never found God unswayed by sincerely held opinion and never distant or unapproachable. Mostly he pictured him as he had since his Oxford days, sitting attentively in a leather armchair in the common room.

"I see now that he is merely a challenge, Lord, a sort of Divine Hurdle that I must leap over or lose the race and I know you can't intend that. I took care, naturally, to give him every opportunity to decide in our favour. I was determined to explore the official channels fully and fairly. After that I simply explained that I had now found an alternative way to finance the restoration of the roof. You see my difficulty was sorting out your will in the general pattern of all the other clues. And now, having done that, I must say that I can only marvel and congratulate you on the sheer ingenuity of it all and Lord I do that humbly and sincerely. Of course we're not out of the woods yet but . . . Ah! Mr. Wilson, no, no please, I had just finished. How good of you to come over so quickly. I've switched to the south chantry as you can see, not quite so much in the front line as it were. How have you been getting on?''

Mr. Wilson nodded dismissively to his ancient workman who melted into the south aisle and away from the problems of others. The architect approached with a considered blend of respect and expertise. Only last week he had told his chairman that the chances of St. Peter's raising enough money to save itself were minimal. William's summons to Flaxfield and his solemn assurance of adequate resources had astonished him, no one knew better how many petitions had been blocked by the Archdeacon. William Coley might well prove to be a Godsend at a time when the building trade was not doing at all well. The vicar was not such a fool as he'd thought but there was no reason why the job should not carry a little extra meat to tide over hard times. If it were done delicately, the original estimate might be revised, perhaps. It was worth trying, and later, with the work well underway, a few corners might be cut with safety and impunity. St. Peter's was, after all, justly famous for the height of its nave. Constant supervision would not be easy.

"It's a question of time, vicar, frankly the sooner we can start the better. I can get a detailed estimate out for you or I can get the construction side of the firm to go ahead before they get tied up with something else. I must be honest, it might exceed my first rough estimate.''

William had developed his second wind, the hurdles no longer puzzled or daunted. Test him as they might he would not be found wanting in courage. He paused to admire Bunter who had flattened his ears and was concentrating on relieving himself into the soft earth above Rupert Corder.

"It must be done," he said, "tell them to start at once."

"I'll keep it down as much as I can vicar, but with costs the way they are . . .''

"You must start," said William firmly. "Can I perhaps persuade you to join us for a simple meal? I'm sure Mrs. Coley would be delighted."

"You're very kind, but with so much to do I think not, please give your wife my regards."

The acrid smell of burnt onion which drifted through the churchyard informed William with practiced accuracy that lunch would be delayed by twenty minutes. Perhaps Mr. Wilson had caught a hint of it before he left but he thought not. The man was without guile. Yes certainly at least twenty minutes, Joan would have ignored a minor scorch, but to have produced an aroma of this intensity could only mean that the onions, and probably the roasting breast of lamb itself, were in flames. Miraculously freed from threat of having to entertain the Archdeacon and his wife and from the complicated horrors of *French Cuisine Made Simple,* her restored confidence had assumed aspects of reckless abandon.

It didn't matter. If the meal was beyond rescue Joan was not a woman to waste time on tearful scraping. No one could fault her when it came to judging the extent of culinary disaster. Scrambled eggs, perhaps? Sometimes they were very good indeed.

"Joan is not an oven cook," her mother had told him when they married and no one ever gave thanks before a meal with more sincerity than William. The fact that she was now approaching him from the vicarage, oven cloth in hand, would mean that she had found herself without any eggs.

"William I am sorry but I'm afraid I've lost the lamb."

"It doesn't matter, we can have something else. Quite lost is it—I mean beyond Bunter even?"

"Oh dear yes, poor Bunter, I'm afraid so."

He linked his arm through his wife's for comfort and led her back towards the house through the sunshine and the gravestones.

"It was my fault, of course, but Mrs. Thomas did rather distract me. She says Lady Ormundham has married again."

CHAPTER 18

"SHE'S HAVING EVERYTHING delivered for June 23rd," Mrs. Thomas informed Webber, as they sat in the shade at the bottom of Doreen's garden. "Coming direct from the brewery in Southwold, beer in barrels and two sorts of wine. I got it from the landlord at the Bull, he's always been very friendly since the funeral. Nothing fancy to eat only bread and cheese, and it's going to be on the lawn in the evening because of the heat. I got it from the girls in the Co-op."

So far, thought Webber, her report, although concise and factual amounted to no more than the preparations for an alfresco party at Henworth Hall. There was nothing to indicate that it had been planned as a background for the public announcement of a marriage. She would have to do better than that. She did.

"They were married last week in London," said Mrs. Thomas with a nonchalant attempt to cross her legs which she abandoned as too ambitious.

"At a registry office. They bought their clothes at Marks

and Spencers in Kensington High Street and spent a night at the Royal Garden Hotel. One of her tenants looked after his horse. I got it from Doreen.''

''How the hell does she know?'' Webber was surprised at the vehemence of his question.

''Mr. O'Shea told her himself. I happened to come back early from shopping when he was there.''

''Well I don't suppose she was best pleased. Weren't they supposed to be having an affair?''

''She didn't seem too upset,'' said Mrs. Thomas. ''Mind you they were both naked at the time. I didn't let them see me,'' she added hastily, recognizing with interest an expression of genuine shock on Webber's face. She shook her head sadly trying gamely to match his mood.

''There's bad blood there, John. She takes after her auntie in London.'' Her solemnity could not be sustained.

''Not a bad report though is it? Fair play!''

When she laughed the ripples came fighting up through her girdle, struggling with her bra and setting her tits quivering like the bonnet of a bus with the engine ticking over in a traffic jam.

''Oh God!'' she wheezed, ''and she thinks she's so clever. That shopping list she gave me was a mile long and she's as mean as much so I knew something was up.'' She wiped her eyes happily but apprehensively.

''Oh dear, don't make me laugh. I must be careful.''

''I'll bet she still hasn't told you what the vicar said to her.''

''No she hasn't, but there's something going on. Have you asked him about the museum yet?''

''He could cover that easily enough. It's interesting but not damning. If he is mixed up in it there's no point in scaring him too soon.''

"She doesn't deserve to get it back, but we're not doing very well, are we?"

"On the contrary, we're doing very well indeed. I'll tell you something Lizzie my girl, you only think that because you haven't got sixteen other cases to worry about at the same time."

"You think he took it then?" Mrs. Thomas quivered like a town spaniel bewildered by the scents of the country.

"Coley? Well he's a good actor but I don't think he's that good."

"But we're doing very well?"

"I think so. I've stopped a few bolt holes; museums, dealers, so my guess is it's got to surface. You see if there's a lot of money bottled up in one rare object the chances are it'll pop up all by itself like a duck in a pond, because it's got to. It's not like used bank notes, you don't often see those again but this is different. I have a nice warm feeling that the Pew Group is about to appear all lovely and clean and laundered, whitewashed ready for the market."

Webber's smile made her feel as young as he suddenly looked. She had been proud of her report but in a curious way, which she could not explain, uncertain of its reception. She only knew that she was relieved that it had not disturbed him. She loved it when she could make him laugh and he looked relaxed and happy as he did now. He was overweight of course and probably eating the wrong things—fried bread, the doctor in Cardiff had been very against fried bread. There was no sense in rushing things which could wait.

His sense of well being and happiness that morning, which reflected his optimism about the missing Pew Group, had arrived at the Bull in the form of an airmail letter from his wife in Corinth in which she agreed that a divorce would be best for both of them. He had not expected it. The subject had arisen years ago when she had firmly rejected it, since when the marriage had lapsed into an irritable acquaintance-ship. Perhaps the Delphic oracle had spoken across the moonlit bay of Corinth and she had succumbed to the charms of the purser or even better a suave confidence trick-ster with his initials embroidered on his shirts. He allowed himself the luxury of imagining her sister's displeasure. She would not like it, and she would say so. Perhaps, he thought happily, they had taken to dodging her on deck.

The Welsh oracle brought him gently back across the sea.

"Joseph O'Shea is a good bit younger. D'you think she's daft?"

"No—no I think she's always known exactly what she wanted. Sometimes you have to wait for things like that. No I don't think she's daft, she's a nice woman." A slight red-dening of the neck was as near as he could get to blushing when he remembered how easily he could have become romantic about Sheila Ormundham. His embarrassment came from the recognition of his naïvety. Inspector Webber should have known better than that. It was John Webber from Flaxfield who had been dreaming alone in the woods again.

Watching him, Mrs. Thomas wasn't quite sure where he'd gone but she had an uneasy feeling that she wasn't with him. She didn't like it when he wandered off like that on his own. Her instinct warned her that an unfavourable compari-son between the frugal repast being offered at Henworth Hall and the lavish, if tainted, provision she had made for Rupert's funeral would be in some sense inopportune and she wisely approached what she had to say from another angle.

"She's ordered special mature cheddar and Adnam's best

bitter, sounds lovely. Will you go if you're asked?'' She had meant the question to sound light and casual but she guessed by his expression that she had betrayed the importance she attached to it so that her added rider was unconvincing.

''I'm not all that bothered myself, it's quite a good repeat on the telly for a change.''

In some ways, he thought, she was like a child with her sudden changes of mood, and she was complex like a child too. Children, he'd noticed, were not often fooled by grownups. They saw through pretence with an ease which had often surprised him when he'd questioned them in the past. It wasn't always as easy to tell when they were lying themselves.

''You do say some daft things sometimes. You know perfectly well we shall both go.''

It was while she was still beaming with pleasure that he suddenly asked, ''Who do you think took that Pew Group, Lizzie?''

He was unprepared both for the speed with which she answered and the identity of the person she named but he listened to her with care and respect. Now that she had been let off the lead, she went bounding around her meadow of speculation, putting up hares only to lose them as her curiosity led her temporarily but deliciously astray. Twisting and turning and retracing her tracks the scent reminded clear and in the end she retrieved her quarry, then, panting with pleasure laid it triumphantly at her master's feet. Webber looked at her affectionately but sadly. It had been worth trying but it wouldn't do.

''It won't do Liz. It leaves too many loose ends. No, it's got to be simpler than that. Motive, that's where it falls down.''

There was a suggestion of movement in the leaves of the

garden like the beginning of a breeze but it lost heart and they were still again. Mrs. Thomas was still too, she did not agree with him but she held her peace.

"Who then?" she asked.

"Goodman—it's got to be. Trottwood knows it too, we've all known it. He's simply found out that he can't get rid of it, it's too hot, even with his contacts, that's why he's gone to ground. Now he's trying to whitewash it through Coley and that's why Coley was talking to Doreen for over two hours."

They fell silent and he smiled at her, softening the blow because he had spoiled her game. "We don't have to wait until the party for a drink, you know. Bugger Flaxfield, come on we'll drive somewhere, there's a Good Food Guide in the car."

From the study window of the vicarage the Reverend William Coley watched them as the car pulled away from the kerb and drove slowly into the glare of the evening sun. Through the glass door of the shop Doreen too watched her mother and Webber until they were out of sight. For a moment it seemed to William that when the car had gone she turned her head and looked directly at him across the empty street and the grave of her husband. He moved back into the room where his white-faced curate was sitting bewildered and miserable on a hard chair. William sat at his desk and broke a long silence by clearing his throat. It was distressing to see the boy jump like that. Now more than ever was a time for cool heads, a time for clear-thinking and courage. No half measures.

"Michael, I want you to know that you are the best curate I have ever had. No priest could be better served. Your loyalty to me and to St. Peter's makes me humble." A hint of colour crept back into Michael Sabini's cheeks. William noted it with relief. If he could instil a little confidence then courage might grow from that.

"I try, vicar. It isn't always easy."

"You have a true calling," said William. "Joan and I saw it at once."

"Sometimes," confided Michael, "even the simple virtues, like honesty, are not easy."

Dear God, what could you do with a boy who believed honesty was simple?

"Honesty," said William firmly, "is a delicate commodity, to be used with circumspection. It should not be bandied about like common coinage." He had no desire to see his curate's gleam of courage dissipated by metaphysics.

"Michael, you have given me your account of the meeting and I accept it without question. You are confusing honesty with truth and they are quite different. Can you imagine that I would have instructed Mr. Wilson to proceed with the restoration if I had the slightest doubt? However bizarre it is patently true, so kindly stop fidgeting with that elastic band and let us go over it again in detail. Now, from your experience of her, would you say that her behaviour on this occasion was a temporary aberration, or has she given you previous cause for concern?"

This was how things should be, Michael thought. A problem shared and discussed unemotionally. At least he hoped the problem was being shared. Sometimes the vicar's reasoning seemed less than clear. He would like to have queried his reference to Mr. Wilson and the restoration but was afraid of looking a fool. However strong your calling it was so easy to feel helpless.

"No, she's always seemed quite sensible before, a little intense perhaps but nothing like this. I once had to make peace between her and Mrs. Willow about the flower arrangements for Easter.''

"No, no," said William, "they all quarrel about the flowers, it is a ritual and never serious unless the church wardens become involved, but the cake is a disturbing element. Perhaps we have missed something significant." He closed his eyes and brought the tips of his fingers together under his chin.

"Very well. Miss Hislop sends you a simple message of great moment, a message she says for the ears of the church alone." He fixed his curate with a solemn stare. "A message for your ears and my ears alone. I'm right aren't I?" he added so sharply that Michael jumped again before vigorously nodding his agreement.

William paused. "I have the Pew Group in my possession and it belongs to the church," he repeated softly in deep concentration. "Just so," he murmured, "just so. An appointment is made, she asks you to call, you accept, she offers you tea and . . . ?"

Michael swallowed hard. "She was apparently quite normal—you know what she's like, bright and chatty."

William's eyes closed again as he inclined his head.

"Well that was the extraordinary thing about the whole time I was there. Whatever she said, and whatever she did, she never altered her voice or her manner."

"Go on."

"She said, wasn't it wonderful about your piece of pottery being so valuable. Then when I reminded her that I hadn't bought it for you but that she'd sold it to the young man with the horse she just laughed and said that was obviously a mistake. What he had really wanted was the bits of brass and she would certainly refund his two pounds and fifty pence."

William swallowed and opened his eyes.

"Was that what she was asking for it?"

Michael nodded. "Actually she said I could have it for fifty pence."

William closed his eyes.

"I thought you might already have it, you see."

William nodded bravely. "And then?"

"Well then, as I told you, she just came out with it."

"On, on!" urged William. "Every detail, we must be exact."

"She was adding hot water to the teapot. She said she saw Mr. Goodman take it from a cupboard when he thought no one was looking. She followed him home and made him give it to her. Mr. Trottwood was already indisposed."

"She blackmailed him you say."

"She didn't mention the word itself, but yes. She told him that she had seen him in the vestry of St. Paul's with that wretched boy. You may remember vicar . . ."

"Yes, yes," said William, "that monstrous child, poor man, no wonder he went away. He had been decorated, I believe, but there are limits to bravery."

"She continually referred to the Pew Group as yours. Do you think she's mad?"

"Misguided perhaps—eccentric even," said William humbly, "but who are we to judge madness, Michael?"

Sometimes, Michael thought, the vicar could be over-charitable. It was no time for reticence. He had asked for every detail and he should have them.

"She was quite plain, vicar. She may have sounded normal but she said it had been defiled and that it must be purified before being offered again to the church. She said the ceremony was well known and quite straightforward. She had buried it in a secret and secluded place from whence, on

Midsummer's Eve, it could be returned after a suitable virgin had been deflowered, preferably by a man of the cloth. And you see, vicar," said Michael, determined this time to make his point, "all this time she kept giving me pieces of cake, and when I had no more room on my plate she deliberately kept putting pieces here," he pointed to his crotch, "piling one on top of the other, and when I protested she said quite naturally, almost as an aside, 'No don't move or they'll fall over' and she was chatting all the time just like an ordinary tea party."

William was silent for so long that Michael wondered if even now he had not conveyed the essence of his encounter.

"As she was balancing the last piece of cake," he said, "she suddenly laughed quite brightly and then she asked if I would care to tango."

William returned to the window thoughtfully. There was no sign of Doreen in the shop doorway.

"It is also known as St. John's Eve of course, for the Baptist, it goes back a long time. Fairies and spirits, bonfires and revels. I can't recall the bit about the virgin. However she is quite well read—mad, possibly—but well read. Sometimes the parish priest was asked to bless the merry-making, she may be thinking of that. Poor woman, she must not be frightened."

He turned to find his curate's troubled and trusting eyes fastened upon him like a child awaiting the end of a gruesome fairy story. Midsummer's Eve, June 23rd, he recalled, was also the night of the party at Henworth Hall, everything always happened inconveniently. However, with courage, nothing was insoluble.

"We must help her. It is our duty."

"We" sounded encouraging. If Miss Hislop was to be

helped it would be nice to have the vicar with him if only as a witness.

"How?" he asked.

CHAPTER 19

By THE EVENING of June 23rd the weather still had not broken. The sun, low in the sky, was a deep orange colour, which became first tomato and then blood as it sank into the highest branches of the trees surrounding Henworth Hall, outlining them against flaming banks of cloud, so bright and vivid that it seemed impossible they would fade and disappear into the darkening blue of Midsummer Eve.

The guests moved about the lawn, sometimes refreshing themselves at the long trestle table or carrying their drinks into the darker light under the trees, to sip and look back to the Hall where the stone walls reflected the glow in the sky, and one of the open doors of the french window on the terrace blazed with the sun itself, as unexpectedly beautiful as the taped music of der Rosenkavalier playing inside the room.

Earlier, after Lady Ormundham had announced that she was now Mrs. O'Shea, Doreen had detached herself from the group on the terrace and, easily outdistancing her mother and John Webber, had sought the comfort of the glooming wood to collect her thoughts. She had found Betsey sitting on a tree stump clutching a pint tankard of beer like a Toby Jug. He would have preferred wine but was too hot to keep walking back to refill the glass and to take a whole bottle he felt would look greedy. She half expected him to tease her, or say something outrageous, so that he would make her laugh and reduce the marriage to kitchen gossip, to be stirred and savoured harmlessly, like paella.

"Come and sit for a bit," he said, gesturing at the grass at the foot of his tree stump. "I'd get down and join you, but with my back I'd never get up."

She settled herself and did as he said. The grass was too dry to make marks on her blue linen trouser suit, and it wouldn't have mattered if it had, he thought, for it wasn't real linen. Some things were important and others not; he wondered if he could ever make her understand that. Faintly in the distance the Princess von Werdenberg was singing her heart out and trying to explain the same thing to Octavian.

On the terrace the lamps remained unlit in the softening light while some of the guests sat listening to the music. Dr. Maguire sipped his wine letting it relax him with the triple pleasure of its quality, the knowledge that there seemed to be plenty of it, and that it was free. If he were younger, he thought, he might well have been tempted to write an interesting case history on his hostess. Interesting, without doubt, but possibly of no great significance medically. "Spontaneous recession of Osteoarthrosis in the hip under the stimulus of emotional and sexual involvement." There seemed to be little doubt that some such thing had happened with her, and yet its application in practical medicine was questionable. The supply of good looking young Irish stallions was limited. It wouldn't last, of course, the novelty would suffer the ravages of wear and tear as the cartilage of her hip had done earlier, leaving her to suffer the pain of both. A stud farm might be the answer, although he doubted if it would receive the blessing of the British Medical Council. Unorthodox treatment had made fortunes before now; a rural setting of charm and solitude, where rich ladies with worn out joints could receive a discreet course of expensive treatment. Perhaps Henworth Hall would come on to the market? Ah! but where would he find his studs? The English were more inhibited than the Irish, and a suitable supply of willing Apollos like O'Shea, with or without butterflies tattooed on their bums, might well be the weak link to shatter the scheme. He compared the mental picture of Joseph stripped for examination in his surgery with some of his village patients of the same age, and the dream faded, the boy was a natural ram, small wonder he'd pulled a muscle; probably Catholic too. It was many years since Maguire had left his native Ulster but the remnants of his Protestant childhood were as ingrained as his love of money.

"Don't you think so, doctor?"

"I'm sorry Mrs. Coley, I was seduced by the music."

"I was saying how beautiful the cheese was, and so fresh. Mine always seems to go waxy in this weather."

"I'm sure this will too," said her hostess, "there'll be so much left over. I do hope you'll take some home with you Mrs. Coley."

William saw an endless procession of cheese pies and Welsh rarebits on burnt toast and he faced it with equanimity. Now that at last the doubt and uncertainty was so nearly at an end he felt that the success of the plan, of which he was but the humble if decisive instrument, would more than compensate for a lifetime of cheddar. The very colour of the sky seemed like a benediction, but he wished he could see

Miss Hislop and Michael Sabini among the figures moving gently about the lawn and the long shadows cast by the nearest trees on the edge of the wood.

"If you'll forgive me, I think I caught a glimpse of Mr. Sabini a moment ago and I really must try and speak to him. No, no my dear," he said pressing down firmly on his wife's shoulder forcing her knees together so that her legs splayed out like a pair of dividers, "stay and talk to our friends, I shall not be long, stay and enjoy the sunset and the music. How lovely it all is, like those wonderful plays on BBC 2; what am I wonder?"

"It would be Chekhov I expect," said Sheila O'Shea. "It very often is, but remember all those servants, vicar. No, I think not, it's just the warm evening and the terrace, but we must all fend for ourselves I'm afraid, the days of bobbing peasants have quite gone."

William nodded happily—he would have nodded happily whatever anyone said—and made for the stone steps leading down to the lawn.

"If you see my husband, vicar," she called, equally happily, "do tell him to come and be sociable. He's gone to feed Katie, but I suspect an attack of nerves. I don't intend," she said to Joan Coley as the vicar pointed into the gathering gloom, "to play second fiddle to a horse. Chekhov is bad enough but I draw the line at pantomime. Did I see you talking to Constable Burnstead earlier?"

"He didn't want to bother you, he runs a small nature study group for some of the local youngsters. He didn't hear about the party until it was too late to cancel it. He was going to ask your permission to use a quiet part of the woods. They are studying bats, I believe."

The light had faded so much that it was difficult for Joan to judge the expression on her hostess's face. Sheila O'Shea was such a pretty name, it would suit her better than Lady Ormundham.

"To be honest I think I've seen them once or twice," said Sheila, filling their glasses. "Only in the distance of course—some of the children seem quite big. It's the wrong Strauss I'm afraid, but I don't suppose they'll notice."

"Unnatural, that's what she is," said Mrs. Thomas, as she watched Joseph adjusting Katie's nose bag. She had soon lost all track of Doreen and Webber and like a child in a fairy story had made for the comforting lights of Joseph's cottage through the dark of the trees. She had not expected to find the bridegroom so far removed from the party, horses had to be fed, of course, she saw that, and she was aware that he and Katie were very close. Would he stable her at the Hall from now on? she wondered. Horses were so sensitive, much nicer than people and so wonderful when they did the show jumping on television. Somehow it was odd to see Joseph in a suit.

The news of Joseph's new social standing in the community had left Mrs. Thomas in a state of some confusion. Joseph, she had decided, was a nice boy and she was delighted both for his good fortune and for the opposing factions which experience told her would inevitably arise in the terrain of Flaxfield and Lower Henworth in general and the Women's Institute in particular. She had determined to align herself firmly on the side of the newlyweds but she would have felt herself to be on safer ground if Doreen wasn't having it off with the groom.

"I could tell you things," she told Joseph, "would make that horse's ears drop off."

* * *

William saw Doreen walking away from the trestle tables with a bottle of wine and two glasses. Their conversation as he joined her was quiet and intimate, inaudible to the few guests who passed near them. Doreen's face remained impassive while she listened.

How lucky we are, thought Mrs. Willow as she watched William's face glowing benevolently in the last of the warm light, such a comfort in times of stress and sorrow, such a fighter for the fabric of the churches in his care, such taste, so wise and certain in his judgment of the flower arrangements.

One minute Mrs. Thomas was puffing along the woodland pathway in hot pursuit of Doreen and then Webber was alone in the gathering night. Sometimes he thought he remembered bushes and trees from his boyhood until common sense told him they had changed their shapes long ago and only the wood itself was the same.

He could still hear the music far away and somewhere there was a sound of distant shouting and laughter. When he stopped and listened it seemed as though the wood was listening with him. Suddenly he heard his own voice calling, unnatural and loud, "Lizzie! Lizzie!"

It was like shouting into a feather pillow.

They had been walking away from the Hall so he turned away from the music and walked towards the distant laughter.

A quarter of a mile to the northeast of the Hall, Miss Hislop and Michael Sabini were pushing their way through quite thick undergrowth. Neither of them was ideally dressed for the route she had chosen yet she seemed quite content to lead the way, and even contrived to lend a certain elegance to their progress, holding back the worst of the brambles with graceful movements of her arm from the shoulder, so that folds of her white muslin dress miraculously remained unentangled and fell to the ground in graceful sweeps, marred only by the occasional intrusive appearance of her brown brogues. Michael, too, had given careful thought to his clothes. He had considered a pair of white cricket flannels and his St. Edmund Hall blazer as being most suitable for the occasion and the heat of the evening, but had rejected them, fearing that such gaiety might convey a totally erroneous impression of acquiescence in a scheme so frightening that he had almost convinced himself that both the vicar and Miss Hislop could only be indulging in a practical joke of such dubious taste, that in their embarrassment they had let it get wildly out of control. This comforting theory had suffered a severe setback when he had called to collect her in his second best dark grey suit and had noted a marked similarity in her costume to that worn by the Vestal Virgins of ancient Rome. Unfortunately he couldn't remember what part they had played in the everyday life of the city; perhaps they were part of mythology and no more to be accounted or believed than the ridiculous rituals of Midsummer's Eve. Certainly, apart from the fact that they were plunging through dense undergrowth in the depths of a Suffolk wood, her behaviour had remained rational in the extreme. She had re-stated her case in the matter of the flower arrangements very modestly, even conceding that Mrs. Willow was showing signs of marked improvement. Not with the roses perhaps, but certainly with her antirrhinums.

A last reluctant bramble released the curate as he followed the billowing muslin into a mossy clearing. Miss Hislop stood for a moment of dreamy triumph. The small trowel with which, on less exotic occasions she tended her window boxes, looked so purposeful and efficient that Michael allowed himself a moment of intense relief. This was where she had buried the Pew Group and now she was going to dig it up without any distressing preliminaries. Faintly through the trees, now touched by the light of an almost full moon, came the pure notes of Octavian presenting Sophie with a silver rose and commenting on her beauty in a distant mezzosoprano.

"How sweet the moonlight sleeps upon this bank," said Miss Hislop firmly. "Here we will sit, and let the sound of music creep in our ears," she added, reaching forward to arrange her dress in modest folds about her ankles, but also removing her brogues and arranging them neatly in a patch of moonlight.

"Antirrhinums," said Michael, in a voice higher than he had intended, "seem to last very well, even in the heatwave." Towards the end of this innocent observation he reached an upper register he had not attained since he had been a choirboy as Miss Hislop gently pulled him down beside her.

"When my first husband was alive," said Sheila O'Shea, "he had an aerial photograph taken of the house and we used it for a Christmas card one year. That sounds so very grand now, doesn't it? Oh, but it was fun! And they took another one, very much higher up, so that you could see all the estate, right out to the Saxmundham road and the house just a tiny speck, like a pinhead. It looked so splendidly feudal, I wanted to send it to all the left wing bigots on the County Council but George wouldn't let me. He thought it silly to draw attention to ourselves; he said that being chairman made it quite difficult enough for him to fiddle his income tax with dignity as it was."

"And will you keep it all now?" asked the doctor.

"Yes I think so, it's not much good for anything really, you know. It would cost a fortune to clear it for building or farming. We couldn't even give it away to the National Trust."

"Nature cures!" said Maguire. "It would make a wonderful clinic! You could sell half of the estate for timber," he said, replacing his glass on the table leaving his fingers free to enumerate his plan. "Sell all your antique furniture and carpets, then modernize the entire house—with taste, of course—as a health farm. There'd be enough to convert one of the old gamekeeper's cottages for you and Mr. O'Shea. It wouldn't trouble you a bit and I," he added triumphantly, "would come and run the whole thing for you. We'd all make a fortune."

"Brilliant! Doctor, you *are* clever, but somehow I don't think I'd like it a bit and I know Joseph wouldn't. He's really rather shy, you know, he likes the peace and quiet as it is. He says he feels safe here. That's odd when you're so young, isn't it?"

Maguire nodded sadly, unwilling to lose his wine dream. "Is he one of a large family? Lots of brothers perhaps?"

"If you were really energetic you could drag him away from that horse and ask him yourself on the way back. Do you think he'll ever make it?" she smiled at Joan Coley, as they watched Maguire weave uncertainly down the terrace steps. "Or shall we lose him at the trestle tables?" She liked the vicar's wife, as a breed they could be meddlesome and overbright but she had always warmed to Joan Coley's pleasant air of vague disaster. "I really don't mind if Joseph stays with Katie," she confided. "You see, I've decided to be very understanding. Do you think," she asked suddenly, "that I've been a fool, a bit pathetic perhaps? People will think it of me, of course, I know that, but I'd like you to say—you don't have to answer."

"No I don't think that at all," Joan paused, looking out to the edge of the light coming from the room behind them. "There's always something, you know," she said thoughtfully. "William is quite obsessed with his pottery and Mr. Sabini, the curate, collects elastic; he has little bits of it all stuck on to cards. We sort out the jumble sales together."

Sheila nodded, the answer seemed to make perfect sense to her. She leaned back comfortably in her chair looking up at the sky and then, in imagination, seeing the wood laid out beneath her like an aerial photograph. A Midsummer's wood; a sanctuary where people talked and laughed and loved to the flight of butterflies and horses and bats, as the Princess von Werdenberg gave the Rose Cavalier his freedom, and far away in the distance came the first faint drum of thunder.

CHAPTER 20

JOSEPH HAD OFTEN received some very stern warnings from mothers, but they had seldom warned him about their own daughters. To be regarded as a newly wed innocent, liable to be led astray by a daughter who was accounted by her mother to be flighty, lazy, mean, heartless and possibly dangerous, was something he had not encountered before.

Not for the first time Mrs. Thomas felt out of her depth. It had never ceased to irritate her that Doreen could so subtly convey the impression that she would be glad to see the back of her. To confess to murder in one breath and then to retract it in the next had been to deny her mother the ultimate position of supreme comforter and protector. For years, both over the telephone, and on too infrequent visits, she had done her best to help the girl with friendship and advice, and now when in her widowhood, and poverty, and perhaps even—in spite of her denials—a murderess, she should have turned to her with gratitude, she had chosen to reject her again and go clattering off up the mountain with a boy on a horse. Ingratitude ranked only marginally lower than murder in Mrs. Thomas's eyes. She had never been able to get close to her and now she wasn't all that sure that she wanted to anymore. Let her get on with it. She would go back to her own life in Cardiff, where she could confide in her friends and describe Doreen's life, not as it was, but as she would like it to have been, so that in time she could come to believe it herself. There had been a moment when she had considered breaking her journey in London and pouring out her troubles to her sister in person but her sister had a distressing tendency to see solutions to problems and acting. On the whole she felt disinclined to give her satisfaction.

Joseph listened to her courteously, he wasn't sure that he understood her intention, and since Mrs. Thomas had confined her tirade against Doreen to a long list of what seemed to him fairly petty grievances, her purpose remained obscure. Fear, more than prudence or maternal affection, had stopped her mentioning murder. She was not certain if, in law, a daughter could sue a mother for slander.

"Ah! Mrs. Thomas now, she's had a bad time; but she'll come through it, you'll see. She has a good eye for the antiques."

He looked at her short plump figure in the cheap cotton dress with green roses on it. They clashed with the pink straps of her bra and the elastic stockinged legs dangling from the kitchen chair he had brought out for her to condemn Doreen in while he was feeding Katie.

"And this heat's a bad time too," he said taking the nose bag off. "I'll look in on her and give her a hand now and then when you've gone." He smiled at her, misinterpreting her silence. "It'll be quiet and lonely for you back home in Wales and you'll worry I know, but there's no need."

182

It was not the reaction she had intended, but she gave up and left the horse's ears where they were.

"She's looks very quiet," she said wistfully, "do you ever ride her?"

"She's a lovely girl," he said cupping his hand to fondle her nose, "and as gentle as a nun. Were you ever a horse-woman, Mrs. Thomas?"

She shook her head. "I watch them on the telly—all the jumping. I think it's wonderful."

Joseph was grateful for the change of subject. "Would you like to sit on her? She'll never move. Wouldn't that be a memory for you when you watch it again?"

Mrs. Thomas's eyes turned from Katie to Joseph and back again and when she smiled it was shy, like a little girl being offered the biggest doll in the shop. Slowly she waddled over to Katie while Joseph brought the kitchen chair over for her to use as a mounting block.

"Never you mind about a saddle now, her mane is as good as reins if you want it, and I'll walk you round the yard. Hitch the skirt well up now to free the legs. That's it! Mrs. Thomas you've a natural seat on you! and isn't that the truth? Whoah! Katie, that's my girl now! No, don't hold her back ma'am, she'll get through that gate and no trouble, she fancies a walk I can see that but I'll be holding her head," he said, vaulting over the paling fence. The slight twist he gave to his ankle on landing was not serious but served to delay him long enough to watch Katie and her new friend disap-pearing purposefully into the gathering dusk.

Betsey sat quietly and listened with fascinated attention to the story of Doreen's renunciation of all her rights in the Pew Group to the church in general and the vicar in particu-lar. Even had she told him earlier he knew now that he could have done nothing to help her. Coley's hand was unbeatable. There was no way she could win unless perhaps . . . As so often in his life Betsey wondered what his formidable mother would have advised. She was always worth listening to.

"Oh come along dear!" said Betsey delicately, fishing a fly out of his wine with his little finger. "Vicars don't threaten people, you've got yourself all upset for nothing. What's wrong in warning you not to repeat that silly story about Rupert to anyone else? I call that very sensible. Anyway he's quite right, who wants the place full of reporters from the Sunday papers? Not that you can believe a word they say," he added scornfully. "Did you hear that? Thunder?" A few leaves moved at the tops of the trees and then were still again, but although they listened carefully the quiet of the wood was unbroken. "All the same it was very generous of you."

She could detect no irony in his voice when he said this, nor when he continued, "At least you should have stipulated that he should give you what you paid for it. Did you know that Midsummer's Eve was the time when you asked for anything you wanted most in the world? It was in a book I got from the library. People used to pray to Satan but then the church took it over in the Middle Ages and tried to make it respectable. Is it my imagination or does it seem cooler?"

"What would you ask for?" said Doreen. "Damn! I'm sorry! What a stupid question."

He held the glass of wine, looking down at it but not drinking. "It's like a part of me inside that's gone," he said after a while, "and I want to be glad but I can't, sometimes I pretend that he's just gone out for a drink and that he'll come back and want his supper. He used to think I hated him for his weakness and failure but I only loved him for it, and he couldn't understand that. I was the safest bet he ever made.'' He balanced the glass of wine with elaborate care on the saw marks of the tree stump.

"You're wrong about Adam, you know. That wasn't my wish. If he comes back I shall tell you I'm glad, but then he might go again, and I couldn't bear this all over again.''

"Freedom is such a silly word, isn't it?" said Doreen, "you need so many other things to go with it.'' She put some spit on her handkerchief and spread the few drops of wine she had spilled on her trousers into a dramatic red blob, like a map of Africa. She looked at it helplessly and gave up. "And if he doesn't come back?" she asked.

"You could try making a thick paste with detergent and leaving it overnight but I don't think you'll shift it. If he doesn't come back," he added, as if it were all part of the same problem and of no greater importance, "I should ask you to marry me and then if you said yes I'd sell the Thatch. It's freehold and worth quite a bit now, I should think. We could use the money to buy stock which is what you need." He didn't mention his mother's money. "There'd be enough to dress you up a bit too. I'd enjoy that, and you would too. You'd have to look your best for all the press interviews, perhaps television even."

"Why on earth . . . ?" Doreen began.

"Because you'd be the news dear, 'Widow of Antique Dealer Left £37 in Will Donates Rare Pottery Group for Church Restoration. A Welsh Angle says Vicar.' You couldn't buy publicity like that. We'd make a fortune. Mummy always said that if disaster strikes you should use it. Make a feature of it, like embroidering a little flower when you burn a hole in a tie. Oh dear, you do look serious! It's only Pretend, you know it can't ever happen. It was just something you said about freedom and I suddenly thought of how it could be for both of us. You can't giggle much on your own and we're not likely to worry about sex unless we both fancied the same one and that's not very likely at my age.''

"I used to wonder if not having children had anything to do with it," Joan Coley was saying to Sheila O'Shea, "but I don't really think so. After all, lots of men collect things and have families as well. How dark it is suddenly. Look, the clouds have quite hidden the moon."

"My first husband collected Dukes," said Sheila. "Sometimes a very poor one would come and stay; he said they were useful on committees. It was a sort of collection in a way, but a bit of a trial for me. Joseph's horse is so much easier. Can you hear them laughing out in the wood? It's been a success, thank goodness. I'll put some more music on and light up the terrace. No, please, I can manage perfectly. Isn't it odd," she laughed, "but it really does all sound a bit like Chekhov doesn't it? Without all the great drama, of course, and not such good food. We must tease Mr. Coley for creating the atmosphere."

William confronted a dishevelled and white-faced Michael Sabini miserably enmeshed in a vicious bramble like a cowardly white hunter in a Tarzan film.

"Please keep your excuses for later, Mr. Sabini, I don't care to hear them now. I cannot believe what you are telling me. I trusted you, and you have failed me. You have also failed your church," he added, visibly struggling to control his anger. "You say she has a trowel with her," he demanded coldly.

Michael nodded wretchedly.

"Kindly direct me to her at once."

When the leaves at the topmost branches of the trees began to move again it was not yet with menace but with supplication, as if they sensed and cried out for relief from the long weeks of arid drought. Small creatures in the tangled growth below sensed it too and waited in the dusty soil with brighter eyes. Constable Burnstead and his eager band pursued their innocent ritual of naked dance and chase among the trees, delaying the sweet passion of fulfilment as if, like all the others in the wood, they too were waiting for the storm. Perhaps because of the tension in the air, or because they had become used to having the secluded estate to themselves, they no longer kept to the remote corner of the wood where Burnstead had warned them to stay, but strayed far from their neat bundles of clothes, running and swaying and leaping as if it were their movements alone which pulled the tops of the trees, making the wood alive and awake after the long days and nights of heat and stillness.

Ambling along a woodland track Katie and Mrs. Thomas shared a similar mixture of emotions. Both were aware that their union was precarious, yet equally excited enough to sense the new spirit of the night, where around the very next corner they would find that the wind had blown the wood clean away, leaving only the open green fields of Ireland or the wonder of Wembley Stadium ablaze with floodlights and the glittering jewels of Her Majesty the Queen.

When the lightning came it sprang down through the trees, not in flashes, but with long fierce bursts of light, brighter than day and more searching than the wind or the huge wet drops of rain which swept aside the leaves and covered the parched ground and every living creature it could reach with splashes as big as saucers, while the thunder ripped and cracked inside their heads like a giant tearing up sheets of corrugated iron. The storm held the wood in its centre, as if unwilling or unable to pass on and let it sink back into the dark until it had stared at everything.

It saw Dr. Maguire standing amazed and encouraged to behold such a wealth of local talent as could sweep arthritis from the land forever.

It watched John Webber ignoring the landscape and lore-leis of his childhood dreams and searching only for a little fat woman with bad legs to comfort and protect her for as long as his heart could beat, be it two or twenty years.

Doreen exploring the farthest boundaries of that elusive freedom, pinned to the forest floor as securely as the butterflies struggling with every thrust to escape from Joseph's wedding trousers.

Miss Hislop and William letting the rain cover them as a blessing in fulfilment, washing away frustrations and doubts as it washed away the earth from her little trowel and from the Pew Group he held high up to the sky to show to the storm.

Mrs. Thomas in Wembley Stadium and Katie far away in the Ireland of her youth but pounding together across the lawn and almost, but not quite, clearing the trestle table to the sound of "Elgar's Introduction and Allegro for Strings." Maguire crying, "she is only winded, stand back! Let her breath! and for God's sake someone get those elastic horrors off!" And Michael Sabini murmuring, "Allow me."

Betsey's dream came true. Surrounded at last by the living proof of the naked naughty witches of his Sunday newspaper dreams, his wig, like his doubts, blown away by the wind that bowled them laughing past him through the magic night and crying aloud for Adam to come and share it.

But Adam never heard him cry out. The storm washed him too, and lit up his face, and the wind moved him in its own private dance as he hung dead from a tree deep in the Midsummer wood.

CHAPTER 21

IT WOULD BE no use, the sale-room expert explained, putting it into a general sale. It would be necessary to wait for one of their specialized sales of fine and rare English ceramics. Only then would they be able to do full justice to such a remarkable example of early eighteenth century salt-glaze pottery. It would also give them ample opportunity for presale worldwide publicity. March 30th would seem the best sale and that would be in about seven months' time. Perhaps, the expert continued, Mr. Coley would care to discuss a few details. There would be the cost of the full page colour illustration in the catalogue for instance, and, of course, the reserve. The reserve, he explained, was the price below which the figure would not be sold.

"Ah yes," murmured William. "I have already taken some advice in that matter," and he happily named the sum he had in mind.

Experts in London sale-rooms are not given to fainting. They are accustomed to thinking in terms of very large sums of money. They do not, as a general rule, expect country vicars to out-distance them in this intriguing pursuit. The expert had been looking forward to a look of amazed and happy incredulity on the face of this gentle unworldly parson, a look such as one might see when a pools winner is told the full extent of his good fortune. In the event the sum named by William was almost exactly double the amount he himself was about to suggest. To his credit he remained outwardly impassive as they both thoughtfully regarded the Pew Group on the table between them.

"It is," he said cautiously, "a great deal of money."

"May I ask," said William, "how long since a similar piece has been offered for sale in your rooms?"

"Not for some years, certainly."

"Ten perhaps?"

The expert looked at William with added respect. He was quite right of course, the years went by and one forgot. His estimate was too low, even so . . .

"And such a lot has happened in that time," William continued gently, "has it not? The price of coffee . . . I have always felt that Pew Groups have been comparatively neglected and undervalued. After all, how many are known to have survived? Twenty? A generous estimate, I imagine. This one interests me particularly in that I can recall no other recorded example where one of the figures is actually touching the lady. Quite provocative in a way, almost saucy one might say, perhaps the word saucy might somewhere be encompassed in the catalogue description?—forgive me, I trespass on your preserve. On the reserve selling price, however, let us stand firm. I may well be wrong, but let us be brave. Unless of course you would like me to place it elsewhere?"

The expert warmed to the kindly naïvety of the clergyman. In his youth he had been much attracted to the church but had decided that it was too unworldly and underpaid. William thought he was a fool.

With the end of the drought Suffolk in general, and Flaxfield together with Lower Henworth in particular, resumed the outwardly unremarkable tenor of rural life, seemingly unmoved by consideration of the current prices in London sale-rooms. A sympathetic coroner's jury had pronounced the balance of Adam's mind to have been sufficiently disturbed to allow William to conduct a burial service at St. Peter's although with the work on the timbers of the roof barely begun it was thought unwise to toll the passing bell or allow Mr. Routledge even the gentlest tribute on the organ, and Adam joined Rupert in the churchyard in comparative silence mourned only by Betsey, together with Bunter and Mrs. Thomas on crutches, past enmities forgotten, united in mutual enjoyment.

By the end of the summer, but before any obvious sign of autumn, Mr. Wilson's men were still deeply committed to seasoned timbers and precise measurements. The scaffolding still supported a weak section of the nave in St. Peter's, the pews were covered with dust sheets and, for the time being, all services were being held at St. Paul's in Lower Henworth, leaving William and Michael Sabini, now reconciled in Christian forgiveness, more time to consider the life's work they had chosen to do their best with. William was much exercised with the parable of the talents and Matthew, Chapter XXV, Verses 14–30, figured very prettily in more than one of his sermons. On fine days the workmen moved about on the roof of St. Peter's wrestling unhappily with the problems of converting feet and inches into the new, unfamiliar metric system.

"Of course Dr. Maguire isn't young," said William,

"but he has enthusiasm and one reads of similar ventures being very successful and the setting really couldn't be better."

"It would be a sort of health farm then?" said Mr. Wilson, as they left the church behind them and sauntered to where he had parked his car.

"On a modest scale at first, a simple regime, fruit juices and so on, with a course of injections, I believe, for a few carefully selected patients he thinks would benefit. Expensive equipment can be added as we proceed and, hopefully, out of future profits."

Wilson found a single loose cigarette in his pocket, pinched out in deference to William's presence before they had inspected the work in the nave. He lit it, surveying William's open face for any flaw concealed in the structure of the fabric and found none. "You mean you're in on it with him?"

"That, odd as it may seem, will largely depend on you."

Wilson concentrated on lighting the pinched cigarette and waited.

"The problem," said William, "is really very simple. We shall form a company. Mr. and Mrs. O'Shea have agreed to let the Hall be converted, but we shall only be able to proceed if Dr. Maguire and I can raise enough between us for the initial venture. I have, as you know, certain expectations. Provided that your original estimate for St. Peter's remained viable and the work completed with expedition, we might well be able to consider going ahead, in which case we should naturally want to commission you to undertake the necessary work. A bare minimum of structural alteration would enable us to open quite quickly, one wing at a time, we thought, and," he added, watching the white September clouds scudding past the deceptively solid outline of St. Peter's, "as with the present work we should not be able to pay you until the sale. It would mean," he said gently when Wilson inhaled in silence, "quite a respectable contract for you."

"This thing—this Pew Group, you really think it's as valuable as they say?"

"Perhaps even more—you must have read the papers—*The Times* itself . . ."

Wilson said, "I remember the place, it's big enough all right, it's not just the conversion you know, you'll need staff, furniture—thought of that?"

"There are things," William admitted, "that the doctor and I had not even considered, such as linen and laundry. My wife and Mrs. O'Shea mentioned them. As for staff, Dr. Maguire seems to think that can be recruited locally, certainly enough to get us started. For a selected number, I confess, the proposed wage seems exceptionally high but I have great faith in his judgment. So you see it really does very much depend upon you, Mr. Wilson. Dr. Maguire mentioned that things in the building trade are rather depressed and we felt you might well consider the proposition favourably. I need not of course stress the confidential nature of our little discussion."

Miss Hislop, like her window boxes, was blooming.

"I'm quite sure you must be very busy, doctor, quite apart from perfectly healthy patients like myself. Never mind, I made sure the tea was ready before you came. Goodness, how exciting it all is! Such an interest for us all, and Constable Burnstead is resigning to join you as security officer, I hear. Do help yourself to cake while I pour. So much for you to think about. And Mr. O'Shea so enthusiastic too, new brooms, it's what we need. There should be a library, had you thought of that? Small but well chosen, you mustn't condemn them to television, you know, and plenty of flowers. I hope you'll let me help if I can.''

Maguire stirred his tea and swam with the stream. He had been in Flaxfield a long time and his interest in her chatter was perfunctory.

His interest in Miss Hislop as a patient, however, was absorbing and passionately professional. If he accepted the result of the tests—and he had to accept it—then, unlikely though it was, this gaunt unlovely spinster with the unmistakable symptoms of incipient arthritis in the knuckles was definitely pregnant. Later, when she could no longer conceal her condition, she could amaze and baffle the wagging tongues of Lower Henworth and Flaxfield to her heart's content. For the moment she was his own treasure, an unexpected and delightful endorsement, a vindication of his most cherished hopes and beliefs. If one brief course of treatment—it seemed improbable that she would have received more—could support his thesis so dramatically, then the future looked hopeful indeed.

"Your information, as ever dear lady, cannot be faulted."

"Mrs. Willow kindly called," explained Miss Hislop.

"Ah!"

"Yes, she wanted to pump me, and lend me a book on Japanese flower arrangements. An unsubtle woman in many ways but we accept each other. She'd been talking to Mrs. Thomas who'd just come from a chat with Mrs. Coley while the vicar was busy with a Mr. Cabert, an expert on antiques from London, I believe. And Mr. Trottwood is to be in charge of all the décor for the rooms I hear, very sound. He has such taste, and designing all the dresses for his wedding too—so very talented, although Mrs. Thomas is not very happy with plain navy and white. She is staying on as chaperone until the ceremony, isn't she? I wonder if she will do the catering?''

Maguire beheld her fondly, much as Alexander Fleming might have gazed upon an early culture of penicillin.

''And the pain in your hand—the arthritis—it really has quite gone?''

''Oh yes, quite gone,'' she beamed at him teasingly, ''and, you see, without any of your strict diet and expensive treatments! Do have some more cake.'' She proffered a plate heavily laden with soggy Dundee cake with one hand. It was rock steady. Maguire observed it with admiration.

''Delicious,'' he murmured. ''Thank you.''

William watched until Eddie's Japanese motor bike with Mata Hari as its pillion passenger turned the corner opposite the shop that sold lawn mowers and disappeared towards Saxmundham and the road to London. How odd women were; she clearly adored the Cabert fellow and yet he had treated her almost like a servant. He hadn't really liked either of them very much and yet they were obviously very knowledgeable and he was committed.

''Lord, I have entered into a business agreement with Mr. Cabert. I did question him very closely, Lord, as you suggested and I must say that such doubts as I mentioned to you after his original telephone call appear to be quite groundless. However, I will just run through it again for you.

''Now, the large reserve price is the figure below which the sale-room will not sell it and that, if you recall, is £30,000. The bidding may not go that high, of course, in which case the Pew Group would be withdrawn and we should have to think again. Lord, I am convinced of its great rarity and value and I believe it will fetch the sum. The sale-room, although rather more cautious, accepts that it is possible, but Mr. Cabert, Lord, goes further. He believes that it will sell for a considerably greater sum and that he can virtually guarantee this. He tells me that it is within his power to ensure that this will come to pass quite legitimately and furthermore that it will be sold to a genuine collector. I confess that I cannot pretend to understand how he can be so certain. When I questioned him he simply replied that it was his job, that it was honest and legal, and that his fee, if successful, would be two per cent of the final bid.''

William paused to allow time for this information to be absorbed and considered.

''I thought it seemed quite reasonable, Lord, for such a service, especially since it appears to be quite honourable. Anyway,'' he ended rather lamely, ''I just thought you ought to know.''

Since no immediate reply appeared to be forthcoming, he rose to his feet with a vague feeling that he had not presented his case as succinctly as he could have wished. Perhaps it was the scaffolding, he thought, as he walked through the nave to the south door, but some of the old atmosphere in the church seemed to be missing.

''Faith,'' he said to Bunter who was waiting patiently for him outside in the sunshine. ''We must have Faith.''

''Jesus!'' said Gaylord Whitman, ''how the hell do you know?''

Eddie sat comfortably in the suite at the Connaught sipping whisky.

''I suppose in a way it's my job. I get to hear a lot of things around the sale-rooms. People think I'm not important, so I listen. It's not always as good as this mind you, but I knew you'd like to hear it anyway.''

"Hell, if he can afford to pay that he might decide to go higher.''

"He can't, he'll be back in Saudi Arabia before the sale. Someone's bidding for him and at that figure he feels he's bound to get it.''

"Oil money," said Gaylord. "Christ, that's all I needed against me. If it was just the reserve price I'd risk it and let the sale-room buy it in and make an offer afterwards, but oil money! Shit, wouldn't you know it?''

"No, I'm afraid it's not just the reserve," said Eddie sadly, "that's why I felt you ought to know. I wouldn't like you to lose it—after all, we sort of saw it all begin didn't we?''

"Eddie, how good is this, how certain are you?''

"One of the porters in the sale-room has a brother, he's a waiter, serves in private suites at the Dorchester. He was quite definite about it. People don't think waiters are important, either.''

"And what's in it for you, Eddie?''

Eddie had already considered his answer to this question. If he had thought his information worth selling to Whitman he would have tried it, but after all what did it amount to? Merely the top price that he would have to pay to buy the Pew Group. Eddie's task was to convince him that he was up against genuine opposition and not just bidding against a high reserve, to push him to the very limit he thought the game would stand. After Gaylord's miserly reward in Flax-field, Eddie would have gladly stung him for more if he could, but reluctantly rejected the idea. He was unlikely to get much anyway, the way the American had been bitterly complaining about the amount of alimony his wife was trying to extract from him; this was the safe and surer way. The man was as mean as muck.

"You've always been very generous, Mr. Whitman, and who knows? I might find something else for you one day." Eddie was quite enjoying himself. "It seems to me," he said judicially as Gaylord poured him a very small measure of whisky, "that you only have two choices. Either the porter's story is true or it isn't. Perhaps it's worth taking a risk and hoping it won't sell, perhaps it won't even reach the reserve if this Arab changes his mind, the whole thing may just be a sale-room rumour."

He happily watched the slow succession of expressions on Gaylord's face as doubt followed hope and was replaced by frustration. But underlying them all was greed.

"Mind you," said Eddie, feeling that his fish had run free long enough and beginning to reel in the line, "with all this publicity there might well be other serious bidders."

Gaylord shook his head. "Not at that price—hell even the sale-room admitted that they felt the reserve price was high at thirty thousand pounds and now you tell me this guy will go to forty."

In the silence Eddie felt his face growing paler and wondered if, in his own greed, he had applied too much pressure and snapped the line. It was too late if he had. He could do no more now, he must have faith, and wait. The winter would come and go and then it would be spring and the time for hope and for things planted now to blossom.

In Flaxfield the days grew shorter and then imperceptibly began to lengthen into the year ahead.

In February the men were well advanced on the work at

the Hall and the church roof was virtually complete. If anything it was more dangerous than it had been before. A single unchecked error in Wilson's original measurements, magnified by metrics, lay concealed beneath the new lead casing, as capricious and uncertain as a child's finger against a row of upright dominoes.

CHAPTER 22

IT ONLY TOOK the television camera crew a few days but it made a charming human interest story; a pleasant end to the late-night news magazine programme, a very refreshing English epilogue to an evening's offering of American corruption and sex, and Irish mayhem and murder.

There were long leisurely tracking shots of Flaxfield basking in the early spring sunshine with the camera pausing to love the old shops and the houses with Tudor bricks and earlier, panning gently through ten centuries in as many seconds, and leading to the newly restored church of St. Peter's where William gave an admirably succinct account of the church's troubles, from the depredations of the Danes and Cromwell's soldiers, to the dry rot which had threatened to complete their work, and the intransigence of certain archdeacons of whom perhaps it would be more charitable not to speak.

The interviewer was at something of a disadvantage. It had long been his established technique to convey an impression of serendipic erudition lightly overlaid by shy charm and pastel pullovers. It was disconcerting to discover that in all three he was easily outdistanced by William, and he wisely decided to be content with the supporting role of acolyte.

"Would you see yourself then vicar as—shall we say—somewhat of a rebel in church affairs?"

The afternoon sun obligingly filtered through an ambitiously purple cloak worn by a Victorian St. Matthew in a west window. It could so easily have come through the lurid green of the grass or the mustard yellow of his halo which would have spoiled the effect of William's close-shot with the silver wings of his hair glowing softly purple with sincerity as though already reflected from an unsought preferment. Tears of pride filled his wife's eyes as they later watched the television together through a light haze of burnt milk.

"No I don't, and you know that's rather a foolish question."

William's quiet smile and expression of gentle affection removed any hint of discourtesy from his reply. "No no, I see your problem, of course." The smile widened boyishly as·he slipped his arm protectively round the interviewer's shoulders and led him through the pleasantly echoing nave. "What shall our story be, you think, eh? The Sydney Smith of Suffolk battling against church bureaucracy perhaps? or the magic discovery of this wonderful Pew Group suddenly appearing miraculously among us like a good fairy or the Holy Grail to save this lovely old church from falling about us?"

The programme cut to a close-up of the Pew Group with a short edited assessment of its rarity and virtues. In the Connaught Hotel, Gaylord nibbled a piece of skin on his little finger and hoped the programme was too late at night to arouse even more competition.

"Your story," said William, as the camera discovered them again in the churchyard, "I suggest, is not about any of these things but about people, and perhaps something we don't hear a great deal about nowadays, I mean goodness, and the goodness of one woman in particular." Miss Hislop gave an involuntary squeak of excitement but William's face faded to reveal Doreen in a simple suit of cinnamon brown surrounded by the combined stock of Trottwood and Corder with Betsey in a new wig doing something effective with a roll of pale blue chintz in the middle distance.

Establishing true goodness on the small screen was solved by allowing Doreen and Betsey to be seen unheard while William's voice explained her sacrifice in detail. They had been interviewed themselves but on playing it back it was felt that she had perhaps not done herself justice while Betsey's occasional interpolations had struck a roguish note curiously at variance with the rest of the programme. There had also been an interview with Mrs. Thomas in which she had traced Doreen's virtues from early childhood in reply to the single question, "What do you think about your daughter now, Mrs. Thomas?" They had kept the question and, dramatically, only three words of the answer. "She's a saint," said Mrs. Thomas in full close-up.

In the next shot the bells of St. Peter's pealed out and Mr. Routledge played the organ fortissimo for the first time since the roof restoration as Doreen and Betsey emerged from the church as man and wife. The vibrations flew through the fabric of the church as they had done for centuries, greeting old timbers with familiarity, setting the dust dancing to the wedding march and bouncing it to the boom of the bells until they rose to the roof shouting the triumph of goodness over greed and evil. The new roof shuddered with incomprehene sion and disbelief and, being attacked from a hundred different directions simultaneously, it became hopelessly confused and remained exactly where it was, thus depriving viewers of an unconventional wedding group, and achieving the first unrecorded miracle of St. Doreen of Flaxfield.

Dr. Maguire felt that it might not have been medically ethical to appear on the programme himself but he lent William his car and some selected facts and figures so that he could be filmed driving out of the village and down the private drive of the estate with his fine head flashing past the rhododendrons until he pulled up at the terrace steps to surprise Joseph and his lady in a carefully rehearsed meeting and be conducted on a brief but delightful tour of Henworth Hall, with glimpses of Katie in retirement, and inserts of Mr. Wilson on the glories of our old buildings and the role of the craftsman in restoring them.

Both Doctor Maguire and Betsey later agreed that William had been nothing less than superb. Whereas the programme could so easily have deteriorated into a dull documentary about a piece of pottery he had, in his no doubt divinely guided instinct, raised it to a higher status of a free commercial for Trottwood and Corder and the Health Farm. Only at the end was the interviewer able to use the Pew Group to tie his final knot for the captions to roll over.

There was a charming medium close shot of William fondling Katie's muzzle in the paddock while touching briefly but effectively on some of the highlights of his recent sermons on the parable of the talents and its significance in the world around us.

"We must never forget that our Lord healed the body as well as the soul."

The interviewer was quite a nice man. Like William he

collected English pottery and although he had not referred to it he deeply regretted turning down the invitation to open the Church fête where Miss Hislop would happily have sold him the Pew Group for fifty pence.

"Vicar, supposing it doesn't fetch enough money to pay for all this?"

William recognized a cue for The Week's Good Cause. "He also said that we must have faith," he intoned, directly into the camera.

Sheila O'Shea switched off the television and refilled Webber's glass.

"Goodness aren't we famous! Isn't it odd how things work out. I never liked it as you know and I believe George thought it was a fake."

"Just as well you didn't mention it on the box," said Webber.

"How awful! Just think of it, can't you see Coley's face and poor Maguire's?"

"Not to mention Wilson—but why did Sir George think that? Did he say?"

"Oh bless him, he got it from one of his pet Dukes to pay off a bad debt. Apparently most of his collection was fake, they found out when he died. He'd been borrowing money on it for years. He sold some of it too, I believe Queen Mary bought quite a lot. Anyway, for once it seems George wasn't cheated. Poor dear, I do wish he'd known."

Privately she thought it was just as well he hadn't known. She had an uneasy feeling that the money would have gone in campaigns to save the village school or more likely poured into a money-losing bus service.

She touched the logs in the fireplace so that the flames danced over the richness and luxury of the room ready and waiting to welcome the arthritic wealth of Maguire's ladies.

For a moment Webber allowed himself to imagine the fireside as his own. Did she sometimes think, he wondered, that her golden airforce boy would now look very much as he did? Probably.

"Doesn't it ever worry you that the Pew Group might not fetch enough to pay for all this? I mean just look at it—all the bathrooms, and that lift."

"No, not a bit." She meant it too, he could see that. "John, I don't stop to think any more, and least of all do I care what other people think, although of course they tell me."

"And what do they tell you?"

"That I'm a brave woman, for one thing. That came from Mrs. Willow at the last Institute meeting but I rather think she meant Joseph. I expect they're busy drawing up the battle lines which means Hislop will be on my side. I like old Hislop. She's quite potty, of course, but Coley seems to have coped very well with her. You shouldn't let me talk so much. How is your new cottage?"

"The garden's a mess. Trottwood says it always gets waterlogged. It wants draining and that could be pricey but luckily Joseph's going to let me have a lot of copper piping he doesn't need any more. The cottage itself is fine, Trottwood sold it as it stood and cheap too. He left everything, carpets, furniture, so I'm in luck there."

"Trottwood's marvellous, just look what he's done to this place. I wish to God I could get him into the Women's Institute. No, I'm mad about him and he copes with Doreen while I manage Joseph. Our main problem is convincing them we don't know about it. Joe's a bigger baby than George was in some ways, he'll make himself sore if he's not careful. I wish I could tell him he can have his cake and eat it."

"And you don't mind?"

"Oh John do be sensible, I'm years older. She's welcome to the steeple chase, I'm grateful for a nice steady canter. Besides he likes me and she scares hell out of him. She won't last, but I will."

Webber chuckled. "Lizzie Thomas would like that."

"Wouldn't she just! Oh dear, I do wish she'd stay. I'm going to need friends."

"I half wondered about offering her a job as housekeeper but I don't know—perhaps not."

"What do you mean, perhaps not. I should think you couldn't do better and you've got plenty of room, it's ideal."

"She might not like the idea—anyway don't say anything. I wouldn't want to embarrass her. I'll sound her out discreetly when I get a chance."

"I'm not very keen on discretion. Action and Faith is far better, you ask my dear Coley—now he does have faith."

"But you don't believe in God, you told me."

"I think he meant in London sale-rooms—oh good! there's Joe, and back early too, isn't that nice?"

CHAPTER 23

THE SALE WAS due to begin on the morning of March 30th at
11 o'clock precisely and at 9 o'clock precisely Miss Hislop
gave birth to twins.

On the whole, the community had accepted her condition
with remarkable composure. There had been early rumblings of rebellion within the Women's Institute which had
been routed by William in a blistering address he had delivered at a monthly meeting. He had attacked on the broad but
topical front of ''Women's Liberation and the Christian
Message.'' Joan Coley had no idea that he held such pas-
sionate views. She wished her father could have heard him.

Michael Sabini had matured visibly; more certain and assured. His respect and admiration for William were close
bounded by secrecy but his hero worship was reflected in a
remarkable series of sermons on service, sacrifice and the
early Christian martyrs. Miss Hislop was assiduous in her
attendance at St. Peter's or St. Paul's whenever he offici-

ated, slowly ripening in her pew through the months until her moment of triumph and fulfilment.

"Two lovely boys," Mrs. Thomas told Betsey, "and no trouble at all, she pushed like a steam roller. My God I wish I had her legs."

"I'm surprised Dr. Maguire didn't make her go into hospital, she must be over 40."

"Thirty-eight; it's in the front of one of her books, 'For Mary on her sixth birthday, September 1946,' *How to Draw Bunnies*. She's kept all her nursery books."

He would miss her when she was gone. He remembered sitting here in the garden with Doreen on the day of the funeral and laughing more than he had for months. Perhaps—given time—he would be able to reconcile them, Doreen and her mother.

"Are you laughing because of Bunnies or because she saved all the books?"

"No, I was thinking about you going home. Most sons-in-law would like that, wouldn't they? You don't have to, you know. You let her bully you too much, she'd try it on me if I gave her half a chance."

She gave his arm an affectionate squeeze and creaked back against the rustic seat. "No, fair does, she wouldn't like it. Shame, really."

"Of course she wouldn't like it, not at first, she'd have to learn, she's been spoiled. The thing is dear, you and I should have been her elder sisters then we could . . ."

". . . Spoil her even more?"

And of course, he thought, since he would be the only sister with any taste or sense of style it would mean double work for him. Still, he would miss Mrs. Thomas. Bunter appeared from some secret access to the main road, intent on his morning round of the most promising dustbins. Either consideration for the occupants of the garden bench, or a lingering memory of the Cardiff ham saved the overflowing receptacle at the kitchen door from closer inspection and he moved on to the rhythm of his planned itinerary, ten minutes ahead of the rural district refuse cart. With tension mounting at the vicarage as the day of the sale approached, regular supplies of food had become even more unreliable than usual.

"She's going to christen them Peter and Paul—so there's no clue to the father there. I asked her right out one night just when she was dropping off. And she said she couldn't remember."

"I knew you'd try, you crafty old devil—aren't we awful, thank God!"

"Mind you, the vicar's had a go too—been with her for hours some nights."

"I don't suppose he's done any better, the wood was full of cocks that night."

The distant clatter of a dustbin lid sounded joyfully on the morning air like a Victorian breakfast gong.

He was right, of course, she needn't even live with them if she sold her own home. There was no reason why she shouldn't be independent. There were too many Mrs. Thomases back there in Wales, the chapel with all its charms was armed with a formidable regiment of well trained opponents; whereas, Flaxfield could really only boast Doreen—the rest were amateurs and ripe for a takeover. She sensed too, a broader outlook, a more sophisticated hypocrisy which appealed to the Latin-American side of her talent for which there had been so little scope in her life, it was time to listen and take courage. He was right. She was wasted in Wales; it was too narrow.

"It's nice here—Rabelaisian."

Betsey blinked.

"In one of Miss Hislop's books," she explained, "she's got some lovely paperbacks."

"A bit strong perhaps? for one unmarried mother I mean."

"It would not have passed unnoticed in Cardiff," she said, "let alone the naughty nudists."

It would be a pity to lose such an ally. In her, he sensed, lay the balance of power.

"There's your sister in London—Mrs. Morgan isn't it?— she'd be company for you, and at least you'd be nearer to us."

The shudder raised the hairs on her legs with such violence that they thrust clean through the elastic stockings. The army in Wales she had coped with successfully for years. Doreen, though a mystery, was merely an interesting challenge, a maverick mercenary. Blodwen Morgan was a general and her territory inviolate, definitely not for living with. You did not tease tigers.

"My sister," she said, as the blood came slowly back to her face, "is demoniac."

As a last resort he was even prepared to disclose his secret bank account but it was unnecessary; she had already decided. It could only be a matter of time before her beloved Inspector discovered he was going to ask her to keep house for him and in that instant she knew she would accept.

"Quite perfect," beamed Betsey, "we shall be invincible."

"He has wonderful plans for me," she confided, "that he knows nothing about."

"That's what I meant, dear," said Betsey.

They sat smiling in happy conspiracy in the spring sunshine. The future was in Flaxfield and there would be a great deal to do. It would be a pleasant surprise for Doreen when she returned from the sale in London with the vicar.

"The ground should have settled nicely by now," she said happily, "we ought to be thinking about headstones."

For the auctioneer it was routine, a perfectly normal sale. From his box rostrum he looked down upon the room with the morning light streaming down from the skylights above. There were no side windows, the walls being covered with paintings and tapestries and pushed up beneath them an assortment of antique furniture for future sales. Immediately in front of the rostrum a horseshoe-shaped table covered in green baize bowed out into the room, and beyond it neat rows of chairs with space for standing room at the back for those bidders who preferred not to commit themselves to a fixed position.

Casual visitors came for a free show, a few more this morning than usual perhaps, attracted by the publicity. Collectors came hopefully. Dealers came seriously and professionally, sitting gravely in their accustomed seats and greeting each other with happy smiles of mutual dislike. On one section of the horseshoe sat the Ring, a few well known dealers who had agreed not to bid against each other for certain lots, hoping to depress the price and buy them for less than their true market value, so that they could bid privately and illegally for them amongst themselves after the sale. Their smiles were friendlier than any of the other dealers. They whispered little private jokes to each other as the lots were passed round the green baize from one to another, pointing out imaginary imperfections in the pieces with eloquent displays of dumbshow disapproval to discourage any collector foolish enough to consider bidding. They beamed at each other in their friendly solidarity and they hated each other most of all.

Gaylord sat on a Queen Anne chair at the side of the room where he hoped he would be able to see who was bidding. He had arranged no elaborate code with the auctioneer. He believed in bidding clearly and openly, and, if necessary, he was prepared to fail. Near him in the centre chairs where his immobility would be plainly observed Eddie sat like a good little boy at Sunday school. Doreen and William, having been photographed by the press as they arrived, now sat quietly in navy blue and clerical grey, like Christian martyrs in the knowledge and love of God.

In the very centre of the first row of chairs carefully dressed to suggest wealth without ostentation sat Mata Hari. It was a perfectly normal sale.

"Lot two hundred and five, the Pew Group." The auctioneer sounded quietly bored. "Five thousand?—Four thousand then."

Twenty-three collectors, two museums and Mr. Inicum began to hope and nod. At ten thousand only the museums, Inicum, and the Ring were left. At sixteen thousand the Ring dropped out. At seventeen thousand Inicum dropped out. At eighteen thousand Mata Hari had beaten the museums and with the bids rising in units of a thousand she began a private duel with the auctioneer until, in less than a minute, it had reached the reserve price of thirty thousand. Behind her thick glasses her face was exactly the same colour as the auctioneer's ivory gavel.

"Any more?" He might have been offering round a plate

213

of bread and butter. "Any more?" It was already more than he had expected. An odd looking woman. Not a face he recognized, the mink looked all right, and the shoes. "At only thirty thousand then." The gavel rose slowly.

Gaylord nodded.

"Thirty-one thousand."

Mata Hari was nodding with such ferocity and speed only because she could feel the chair beneath her moving like water and she was desperately anxious not to faint before she reached the magic limit at which Eddie had said she could stop.

"Thirty-nine thousand." She stopped. So did Gaylord.

"At thirty-nine thousand." The auctioneer politely offered the pause to Gaylord. "It's against you sir." He didn't move. Eddie watched the gavel rise like a blade on a guillotine.

"In the centre of the room then, at thirty-nine thousand pounds."

Before the descending ivory could smack on to the wood of his rostrum the auctioneer caught Gaylord's last nod and he had bought the Pew Group before the waters rose above the pebble glasses and the hired mink had cushioned Mata Hari's fall.

There was no way of telling what had happened to the new timbers inside the roof of St. Peter's. By every known law of man and God they should have supported nothing and destroyed everything. Only the last faint rumblings as they locked into inexplicable security disturbed the small bird which had started to build its nest again in a sheltered corner near the tower. It flew down into the churchyard for safety.

After William's telephone call Joan Coley set out to be the first to give the news to Betsey and Mrs. Thomas. At Rupert Corder's grave she was confronted by Bunter washing with gratitude beside a few crumpled feathers.

You couldn't call it murder and he had no intention of doing so.